THE STAIRS BETWEEN US

ELIZABETH BARONE

ALSO BY ELIZABETH BARONE

MAIETTA INK

The Stairs Between Us

Copyright 2018 by Elizabeth Campbell, writing as Elizabeth Barone

All Rights Reserved

1st Edition

Cover photography by Artur Verkhovetskiy

Cover designed by Natasha Snow Designs

ISBN 978-0-9912838-4-2

❀ Created with Vellum

THE STAIRS BETWEEN US

After you get divorced, you're supposed to walk away. Neither of us could.

It's been a year since Noah left her husband, and she's drowning. Between raising her son and chasing her dreams, there just aren't enough hours in each day. Noah needs a teammate, but her ex-husband is married to his job, and that will never change.

Levi lost his whole world when his wife left him. He loves his family and loves being a surgeon, but couldn't commit to both. Now he comes home to an empty house—a reminder of the promises he broke and the family he lost.

Noah and Levi move into the same apartment building just to help each other out. With only a flight of stairs between them, though, they could be closer than ever before—if they'll just meet each other halfway.

JANUARY

❧ I ❧

NOAH

The early morning glow filtered through the blinds—the wrong kind of light. It should've tipped me off, but it never did. I rolled onto my side to face him, a hand automatically stretching out. My fingers touched cool sheets.

Empty bed.

No husband.

There were still mornings when I woke, half expecting to find myself in my husband's house, in our bed. Most mornings, actually. I should've been used to it, but somewhere between sleep and the land of the living, my brain kept glitching out.

Levi always kept blackout curtains in our bedroom. Those sheets never saw the light of day. With his odd hours, he needed to be able to sleep no matter what time of day.

I squeezed my eyes shut, willing myself back to that bedroom, to that life. To the person that I was. The velvet inside of my eyelids glowed red from the diffused light, the illusion shattered.

Even though I'd divorced my husband, I still missed him.

No matter how much I missed him, though, I'd had to leave.

I glanced at the alarm clock on my nightstand. I didn't have to get up for another fifteen minutes, but I couldn't go back to sleep.

My brain already ticked through each thing I had to do for the day, a perpetual running list that never shut up—even while I slept.

Running feet pounded the carpeted hallway as my six-year-old son zoomed toward my room. He flew through the open door and bounded into bed with me.

"Good morning, Momma!"

Pushing away all of my worries, I snuggled him into my arms. "I love my cup of morning Joey." I inhaled the scent of his mousy brown hair, breathing in the scent of sleep and berry kids' shampoo from his bath the night before.

"Am I going to Daddy's today?"

"Tomorrow, buddy." I hugged him tighter. "Today's Friday."

Joey giggled. "No, Momma. Today's Saturday."

He was right. I threw on a smile to hide my grimace. "Are you sure? I can still bring you to school." My fingers found his ribs, tickling lightly.

He squealed, wriggling away from me. "No school. I want to go home. I mean, to Daddy's." He studied my face with dark eyes that were so like Levi's, waiting for my reaction.

"Daddy's house is your home, too," I reminded him. My heart throbbed with guilt. What I did hadn't been easy on my son. As much as I missed Levi, I knew Joey missed the three of us being together even more, no matter how much of a brave face he put on.

"Why . . . ?" His voice trailed off.

"What, buddy?" I sat up in bed, tendrils of dark hair reaching down my back, tickling my skin as they tumbled over my shoulders.

"Never mind," he mumbled. His eyebrows remained pinched together, though.

"Honey? Talk to me." I stroked his smooth, creamy white cheek with my thumb.

"Why can't we go home?" Those round brown eyes stared up at me.

"We *are* home." I gathered him into my lap. "This is my home, and Daddy's house is his home, and both of those places are your home. Remember?"

Twisting in my arms, Joey came face to face with me. "Seems like a lot of homes."

I chuffed a tiny laugh through my nose, a smile touching my lips. That was another way that Joey was like Levi. They both thought logically. All of the pieces needed to fit, no room for arguments or emotions. Sometimes I wondered if this boy was even mine. The only physical feature he'd inherited from me was my chin. My sapphire eyes skipped him, and his genes took off running after his father.

"Sometimes mommies and daddies need to have more than one home." I patted his leg.

"Yes," he said, as if explaining to a toddler, "but one home costs less money."

"I know you want things to be the way they used to be, but we're still a family."

Joey slid out of my arms and off the bed. "We have a *lot* of bills." He turned and padded toward the hall in his bare feet. "Can we have pancakes?" he asked over his shoulder as he ambled out of sight.

I sighed. Even though he was only six, he saw and heard everything. He noted the bills piling on the table, some with red PAST DUE stamps, and assembled the pieces. Just like he saw Levi's empty kitchen table, the mortgage already paid off and the bills automatically withdrawn from his checking account.

Leaving my husband had cost me more than I'd been prepared to lose.

Life went on, though. It had to. If I spent too much time assessing my decision, I might doubt it. And I didn't have room in my life to start second-guessing myself.

The damage was done, as they said.

I climbed out of bed and wrapped myself in my thick flannel bathrobe, tucking my feet into slippers. As I moved through my room, I glanced out the window. Part of me hoped that I'd see snow on the ground, January continuing its pattern of dumping snow on our small New England town just so I could keep Joey for one more day. No such luck, though. Both the sky and streets were clear.

That soft morning sunlight kept on shining.

On Saturday mornings before it all fell apart, Levi let me sleep in. I'd wake up to coffee in the carafe and my husband flipping omelettes on the stove. I'd hop up onto the counter, he'd hand me a plate, and I'd wrap my legs around his waist. Then I'd feed us both little bites while we talked about our dreams and laughed.

Sometimes dreams can turn into nightmares, though. You can become consumed by what you think you want, until your view of everything around you slowly narrows and you lose sight of what's important. The people you leave behind are forced to pick up the pieces, to make the hard decisions.

I couldn't explain these things to my son, though. At only six, his world view was simple: mommies and daddies stayed together. At least, his were supposed to. No matter how many times I read him children's books about divorce, or how many kids in his first grade class told him their parents separated too, Joey would always want us back together.

I couldn't blame him.

No matter how much time passed, part of me would always long to be back in that house. The days I longed for, though, weren't the later years of our marriage. I wanted to return to before Joey was born. Not because I didn't want my son, but because I wanted the man I'd married. The man who held my hand on our walk over to campus, who slipped sweet little notes into my backpack.

I wanted the Levi who looked at me as if I was his whole world, his brown almond-shaped eyes filled with the dreams he had for us. The Levi who saw the whole picture and wanted to keep looking.

That Levi was gone, though, replaced with a cold lookalike who barely saw me when he bothered to come home. The doppelgänger who came home from the hospital hardly glanced at our son, ignoring his pleas to "Come play dinosaurs with me, Daddy."

I shuffled into the kitchen where Joey already stood on a chair at the counter. A mixing bowl and the box of pancake mix sat in front of him.

"I waited for you," he told me.

Kissing the top of his head, I grabbed a measuring cup. He was already six. There weren't too many pancake mornings left, fewer still afternoons spent playing with dinosaurs in a sandbox.

Whether you paid attention or not, time kept moving forward.

"Wanna stir?" I asked my son. He nodded and I handed him a rubber spatula. "Go for it."

"Momma," he began as I poured water into the mix.

I paused, holding the measuring cup over the board. "Yeah?"

"You're putting too much water."

Peering at the pancake mix and the water already in the bowl, I shook my head. "Honey, I've been making pancakes since before you were born."

"Momma," he said again. "It's a two to three ratio."

I blinked at him. "It's a do what now?"

Joey sighed. "It's one and a half cups of water for every two cups of mix." Gently, he took the measuring cup from my hand and set it down. Then he grabbed the box and pointed to the chart on the back. "See?"

Shaking my head, I moved toward the coffee pot. "I'll just let you handle that, then," I told him, reminded again of how like Levi he was. Math and science—those came easily to the men of my heart. When I made pancakes, I just added water until the batter was right. When Levi made them, the measurements had to be exact.

Precision made for a fantastic surgeon. Surgeons made for terrible spouses. I just hoped that Joey wouldn't take after his father in that department, too.

✿ 2 ✿

LEVI

Wind whipped around the corners of the house, creating an eerie howling effect. I sat in the kitchen, listening more to the wind than to the guy I called my best friend. Guilt picked at my stomach, making it acidic. I should've been making an effort to be there for him. The only thing I could focus on, though, was the time ticking closer on the wall.

"I think it might be stress," Theo said in his soft-spoken voice. It was hard to believe that a nearly seven-foot man could have such a gentle voice. He spread his dark hands. "Pamela's got her hopes so high, and she gets so frustrated." He cleared his throat.

My gaze snapped up from the kitchen table. I met his brown eyes across the table. "Sorry, man."

"Is Noah dropping off Joey this morning?" he asked.

I nodded, rubbing the back of my head. "Any minute now."

"I guess there's no chance in me stealing you for a run." Theo grinned, and for the first time I realized he wore his running gear.

I glanced down at my long-sleeved henley and jeans. Maybe I would've been better off throwing on sweats. I no longer had the effect on Noah that I'd had on her in college, but I still tried.

6

It was pathetic.

"A run might help get your mind off things," Theo said, his voice returning to that lulling level.

"Yeah," I agreed, "but I can't leave Joey."

"I'm sure Pamela wouldn't mind looking after him."

I laughed, the sound bitter. "And have it get back to Noah that I dropped my kid off on someone else the second he got here? No thanks." I rubbed at my beard. "How did I get here, man?"

"It takes time." He stood to his full height. After over ten years of friendship, I was used to him towering over me. At UConn, people called us Sully and Mike when we walked around campus together. He'd go to basketball practice and I'd head to my premed classes.

Or the poetry class where I'd met Noah.

Together, though, Theo and I were a duo. When people threw parties in their dorms, they told each other: "Make sure you invite Sully and Mike."

College. Those were the good days.

The doorbell rang, yanking me out of my thoughts. Standing, I tried to arrange my features into what I hoped was a relaxed expression. Instead, my brows rested heavily over my eyes as I made my way to the front door. Taking a deep breath, I swung the door open wide.

"Daddy!" Joey threw himself into my arms.

I scooped him up, hugging him to my chest. "Hey buddy." Over his head, I glanced at her.

Noah.

A full year had passed since we separated, and six months since the divorce was finalized, and still just the sight of her knocked the air out of my lungs. She lifted her angular chin, sapphire eyes looking at Joey and me but avoiding my gaze. She nibbled at her full, pink lips.

Releasing Joey, I fought the urge to embrace her, too. My ex-wife. I still couldn't get used to the phrase.

"Uncle Theo's in the kitchen," I told our son.

Joey's eyes lit up. Dropping his backpack in the entryway, he took off toward the kitchen.

"This isn't a dumping ground!" Noah called after him. Her eyes sparkled with amusement, though.

A year earlier, this had been our home. Yet there she stood, in the doorway, half out of my life.

"Want a cup of coffee?" I asked, shoving my hands into the pockets of my jeans. Cold air swirled around my bare feet.

"I should go." She jerked a thumb toward the car idling in the driveway. When she left, she didn't even keep the car I'd bought for her. She drove a brand new Toyota Camry that she was probably leasing—and paying out the nose for every month.

I didn't get it. She could've kept the Jaguar. I'd bought it for her.

"It's cold," I said. "Just come in for a few. Run me through school?"

For a second, her eyes lit up. Then her lips tightened. "I've got lesson planning to do." She turned, low ponytail whipping around through the bottom of her beanie.

I closed my eyes. I'd meant *Joey's* school, forgetting entirely that she'd started grad school—all while caring for our son and teaching English at the high school. "Wait," I called. "How's business school?"

She paused, boots crunching over the salt on the shoveled front walk. Turning, she shoved her hands into the pockets of her coat. Her eyes lifted, but still didn't meet mine.

When I breathed in, my chest ached. Without her in my life, I rattled around in my body, in the big empty house we'd once shared. Though she haunted me, I was the ghost.

"Demanding," she said. "I've gotta go." She hesitated as if she had more to say.

"Noah . . ." A thousand questions burned on my own lips. Even after all those months, I still didn't know why she left me. I'd thought we had a good thing going. Sure, my job could be demanding. I was the best pediatric urologist in the region. Those kids needed me, and I couldn't exactly ignore my pages. I knew Noah wanted me home more, but I thought she understood.

Until I came home to a dark house.

"Can you drop him off tomorrow night?" she asked, eyes on my beard.

I suppressed a grin. She'd always liked when I went without shaving for a few days. I was pushing dress code at work, but seeing the look in her eyes was worth it. "Of course," I said, voice soft.

"I would just get him myself, but it'd buy me some extra study time."

"It's no problem." I swallowed, and stepped onto the porch. "Look, Noah, I can take him for the week, if that helps."

Those triangular eyes narrowed. "Our current custody agreement works just fine."

"I know," I said quickly. "I just meant, if you need me to step up to sixty/forty custody, just to give you more time for school—"

She laughed, a short, bitter bark. "How exactly would that work? Are you going to take a vacation?"

I licked my lips. "I'm trying to help."

"Or are you just going to send him to your mom's?" She clenched her keys.

Jaw tightening, I sucked in a deep breath. "I'm just going to finish my coffee," I sat flatly. "I'll see you tomorrow night."

"Great," she said. She turned, boots scraping against the ground. Her heel spun, sliding over a small patch of ice that the snow removal guy had missed. Legs flying out in opposite directions, she started to fall.

I jumped down from the porch, bare feet slapping against the freezing cold walkway. Pebbles of salt bit into the soles of my feet. Arms outstretched, I reached for her. I hooked one arm under her bottom, wrapping another around her shoulders, and drew her into me.

We both went down.

I landed hard on my back, the air exiting my lungs in an icy whoosh. My body absorbed the impact, and I cradled Noah in my arms. With a grunt, I met her eyes.

Only inches separated us. Those blue eyes stared into mine, both wonder and fear mingling in them. I frowned. She had nothing to fear from me. I would never hurt her. Both the oaths I'd taken bound me from harming her: the Hippocratic Oath, and my marriage vows.

Even though our marriage was technically over, I'd never break them.

"Are you okay?" she whispered. Her breath warmed my face.

"Yes," I rasped. I tried to suck in a deep breath, but my lungs were still in shock.

A strand of hair escaped her beanie, caressing my cheek. "I'm sorry," she said, lips so close to mine, all I had to do was lift my head.

"Good thing," I panted, "I'm off today."

"Good thing you're a doctor." A corner of her mouth lifted. "Tell me what to do for you, Dr. Wester."

Come home, I wanted to say. As my lungs started working correctly, though, I realized my arms were still around her—my hand still on her ass. I loosened my grip, releasing her.

She brushed snow out of my hair. "Thank goodness your head landed in the snow."

I glanced around. Sure enough, we'd twisted as we fell. The snow wasn't exactly soft, but it'd saved me from cracking my head open on the pavement.

Noah rolled off me, and my body instantly went cold without her. I sucked in a deep breath to salve the ache in my chest. She stood, holding her hand out to me.

Reaching for her, I braced my elbow against the walkway, pushing off as her hand closed around mine. I outweighed her by at least 100 lb. "Thanks."

Biting her lip, she walked around me, evaluating. "You look okay to me, but you fell hard, Levi."

"I'm fine," I lied. "Really. It's nothing a little Advil can't fix."

Most of the damage wasn't physical, though. All of the painkillers in the world couldn't help me, not with Noah out of my life.

"Theo's inside, too," she said, as if reminding herself that she had no obligation to stick around and nurse me.

"He's going to be devastated to hear that I won't be running with him for a while." I shooed her. "Go. We'll be fine."

"Okay." Her eyes flicked up to mine for a moment, then darted away. Without another word, she moved carefully down the driveway.

Just like in our divorce, I'd absorbed the impact. Noah always got away clean, leaving me to lick my wounds. Before she left, all I'd wanted was a family and a career, but I couldn't juggle the two. After, I'd thrown myself into work, dropping the ball as a father in an effort to save my patients and give my son everything he wanted. Sometimes I thought I'd never find the right balance.

❈ 3 ❈

NOAH

I took a deep breath for the fifth time, steadying myself as I sped toward my best friend Pamela's house with Eisley on full blast. With her husband Theo at Levi's, I only had a short window. I needed girl talk, stat. My favorite band could only ease the pain so much.

Even after a year, Levi could knock me off my feet *and* catch me in the same moment. My skin still burned from his touch, the layers of clothing insignificant.

I'd had to go, though—no matter how much I missed him. The old me would've laughed and started a snowball fight. Levi would've dragged me into the snow with him, flakes coating our hair and clothing. Then he'd lean in, the laughter dying from my lips, and press his warm mouth to mine, tasting me slowly.

I had to clamp my thighs shut while driving, just thinking about it. I could actually feel the scrape of his stubble on my skin.

Pulling into Pamela's driveway, I threw the car door open before the car rolled to a complete stop. Her driveway looked dry, so I hurried to the garage door and punched in the code. Seconds later, I stood in her kitchen, the warmth of the floor seeping into my socked feet.

"Honey, I'm home," I called.

"Upstairs!"

I found her in her bedroom. She sat crosslegged in sweats, her fiery red hair pulled up into a messy bun.

"Stay back," she said, holding out a hand. "I've got a cold."

"Googling home remedies?" I nodded to the laptop in front of her, then plopped down on foot of the bed.

"Sort of." She squinted at me, her hooded brown eyes studying me. "What are you doing here, anyway? I mean, I know we have an open door policy, but it's a Saturday. Weekends should be crisis-free."

"Ha." I traced the snowflake pattern on her duvet. "I just dropped Joey off."

"Oh." She closed her laptop. "What happened?"

"Levi offered to take him more, so I could get my schoolwork done."

"That doesn't sound so bad," Pamela said.

"No," I agreed, "but where was that team spirit before?" I sighed. "I guess I just miss having that team unit, you know?"

She nodded.

"I mean, I know I have you, my sister, and my parents, but . . . it's not the same. Even when we were married, it was mostly me. The more successful he became in his career, the less *I* had him."

"I know." Pamela gently touched my arm. "It's good that he's trying now, though, isn't it?"

"For how long, though? You and I both know that his schedule is all over the place. I'll be lucky if he doesn't call me tonight, telling me he's been paged." I rolled my eyes.

"Well, if that happens, Theo and I are more than happy to take Joey." She looked away, worrying her lip.

"I appreciate it, but you guys aren't Joey's father. He hardly gets to see Levi as it is," I said, trying to draw her back into the conversation. Pamela nodded, but her eyes remained distant. "What's wrong, Pam?"

She smiled, gaze returning to mine. "Just that balloon head feeling. I'm fine."

Poor Pamela. I needed to make her feel better somehow. "I fell on top of Levi," I blurted.

"What?" Pamela scooted closer, her eyes widening and mouth dropping open. "Spill, now!"

I filled her in, only leaving out my conflicted feelings.

"So what does this mean?" she asked, reaching for a tissue.

"I'm clumsy." I shrugged.

She blew her nose, crumpled the tissue, and tossed it into a basket. "Score," she muttered.

"Do you and Theo turn everything into a basketball game?"

"You can't distract me." She crossed her arms. "I see that look on your face. You miss him."

"Of course I miss him, Pamela. We were married for nine years. He's the father of my son."

She looked away, sniffling.

"That," I said, snapping my fingers. "That's what I'm talking about. Are you sure you're okay?"

Her lips twisted to the side. Slowly, her brown eyes lifted to meet mine. "I do have a cold," she said, "but it's not just that." She took a deep breath. "Theo and I . . . are trying. It isn't working, though."

I touched her knee. "Aw, Pam. Why didn't you say something? Here I am, going on about nothing. How long have you guys been trying?"

"A couple months." She pulled her hair out of its messy bun. Red hair spilled down her shoulders, but she scooped it up quickly, smoothing flyaways and putting it into a neater messy bun.

Squeezing her knee, I smiled gently. "A couple months is nothing. You were on the pill, right?"

She shook her head. "IUD."

"The one with the hormones? It takes time for your body to readjust, to get back into its rhythm. It took me months to get pregnant with Joey. It gave Levi and me plenty of time to practice, though." I laughed, thinking of the moment when those two pink lines had shown up, how Levi asked if we could practice just one more time.

"You're probably right," Pamela said. "I guess I just had this vision of getting that thing out and getting knocked up right away."

"Plus," I said delicately, "we're twenty-nine now. We don't get knocked up at just the sight of a penis."

Pamela shoved me gently. "Noah Wester," she said with a laugh.

"It's Clarke now," I reminded her.

"Right." She studied me. "I can't believe I'm asking you this, but don't you want more kids? A little brother or sister for Joey?"

I sighed. "That ship has sailed, Pamela. Which is why you have to give him five little cousins." I slid down from the bed. She might not be related to me by blood, but she was my other sister, as far as I was concerned.

"Five?" She fanned her face with a hand.

"What?" I asked innocently. "I thought you always wanted a big family."

"Yeah, but *five?*" She shooed me. "Let's talk about something else before you jinx me. How's that book coming?"

Groaning, I closed my eyes. "It's not."

"Did that writing book that I gave you help at all? The one about psychology of story?"

I covered my face with my hands. "No," I said mournfully. "It's excellent, Pam. It really is. I was already overthinking everything, though."

"Well," she said, a sly smile spreading across her face, "it takes time for your brain to get into that writing rhythm. Think of this book as practice. I'm gonna need five book babies on my desk by the summer, though."

I tossed a throw pillow at her. "Touché."

BACK IN MY APARTMENT, I TRAILED THROUGH THE ROOMS LIKE A ghost. Levi's and Pamela's houses made my place look like a dump. It wasn't, by any means, but the five-family home I lived in was over a hundred years old and in desperate need of repairs. However, my landlord ignored each of his tenants' complaints. I stood in the bathroom, nudging at the kick molding with a toe. The piece threatened to come off completely, and I didn't want to know what it'd reveal.

Once upon a time, it'd been a beautiful house. More like a mansion. There weren't many apartments available in Watertown, so I took what I could get. It wasn't perfect, but I was a little broken too. Eventually, I hoped to buy one of the condos on Cherry Avenue. As a high school English teacher, though, I'd be lucky to afford even that on my own.

I was supposed to be working on school stuff, but with Joey gone, the apartment echoed around me, too empty. Still, I had a limited amount of time before Levi got paged into the hospital for an emergency. I should make the most of it.

I opened the laptop still on the kitchen table, torn. Even though I technically had an assignment due for my grad program, or should at least be working on lessons for the next week, the novel sitting on my hard drive called to me.

I'd always wanted to be a writer. Instead, I swam around it, blogging about YA books and teaching literature to high school students who didn't always care. When I left Levi, I could've crumbled, clinging tighter to my job at the school. Instead, I saw only a wide open door to opportunity. I started writing the book that had lived in my heart for years, and enrolled in an online grad program for business and marketing to kickstart my new writing career.

I'd never lived on my own, nor had I truly felt in control of my life, but there I was. No matter how much I missed having someone to come home to, that kind of freedom was priceless.

It wasn't enough, though. It never would be.

4

LEVI

"Well, I'll leave you to it," Theo told me. He ruffled Joey's hair with a large hand. "Ice skating later, little man?"

"Yup!" Joey grinned. "I've been practicing."

"Yeah? With your mom?" Before I could stop it, a memory of Noah gliding in a slow circle played across my eyes, a tape without a stop button. Even the way her jeans hugged her ass was imprinted onto my brain forever.

Joey made a face. "Momma can't skate. I watched it on YouTube."

A laugh rumbled out of Theo's barrel chest. "That ain't practicing, dude." He shook his head at me.

"I know how to skate," Joey insisted, the smooth skin between his eyebrows furrowing.

"Sure," I said.

Theo ducked out of the kitchen, his laugh trailing him all the way to the front door.

"You know," I told my son, "your mom does too know how to skate. We used to go all the time, before you were born."

He raised a skeptical eyebrow at me, looking so much like her in that moment, my chest tightened. "Didn't she just slip on the ice outside?"

My heart hammered against my sternum. "You saw that?"

Joey pushed his chair back from the table. "May I be excused?"

"Hold it, buddy." I dropped to one knee, meeting my son's eyes. "You wanna talk about it?"

"Are we moving back in?" he asked, expression still dubious.

I rubbed the back of my head. In some ways, Joey was still having just as much trouble adjusting as I was. I didn't know how to answer him, though. No way was I going to give him some bullshit response, but I didn't want to blow him off, either. Not like my own father. "I don't think so," I said at last, opting for honesty.

Joey's head lowered slowly. He stared at his hands in his lap.

Though it wasn't anatomically possible, my chest tightened as if my ribs had constricted around my heart. A flash of anger slashed through me—anger at Noah, but also at myself. My whole life, I'd promised myself that one day I'd have a family again. History wouldn't repeat itself. Yet there I sat, having a conversation with my son so like the one I'd had with my mother.

The only difference was, I'd never leave my son—no matter how much Noah had hurt me.

"This is my home, too," Joey said, round eyes meeting mine again. "Right?"

"Of course." I touched his cheek. "We're still a family." My voice nearly broke on the word. "This is still your home."

"Can we get a dog?"

"Ah," I stalled, fighting a smile. "Since when do you want a dog?"

"Momma says the apartment is too small."

"So you thought you'd ask me." I nodded, mulling it over. Even if Joey lived with me full-time, I couldn't care for a dog. Not with my schedule. Telling him no would crush him, though. He'd already been through so much. "Tell you what. Let's talk about it." I stood from my crouch, and eased into a chair.

"Okay." Joey folded his hands on the table. "I want a German shepherd."

"You've really put a lot of thought into this." I flipped a pen between my fingers, sitting back in my chair. "Shepherds have a lot of energy. She'll need to be walked a few times a day."

"She?" He lifted an eyebrow at me.

"The dog. Can you come here twice a day and walk her, even when you're at Momma's?"

Joey's eyebrows knit together, making his elfin face look older beyond his years. I could practically see the wheels turning. Then he sighed through his nose and looked away.

"It wouldn't be fair to the dog," I explained.

"You said 'she.'"

"What if we got a really cool cat? One who could play fetch?" I tapped the pen on the table, then released it.

"You want a dog, too," Joey said.

The corner of my mouth twitched. "What makes you say that?" Sometimes I forgot how perceptive my son could be.

"You could've said 'it,' but you said 'she,' like you're imagining having a girl dog." Wise brown eyes met mine.

I cleared my throat. "It would be really cool to have a girl dog," I said, thinking of Heidi, my childhood German shepherd. It was possible that Joey had seen a picture of her and remembered it subconsciously, but I didn't think so. He just knew things sometimes.

I couldn't admit to him that I had the same picture in my head. Except, in my version, Noah hadn't left me. The three of us stood around a sable German shepherd, maybe even a tiny baby bump in Noah's belly.

"It's okay, Daddy," Joey said, resembling a six-year-old again. He slid down from his seat.

"So you don't want a cat?"

As he opened his mouth to answer, my work phone buzzed with a page.

"Hang on, buddy."

"It's fine, *Dad*," he said, turning away.

"Wait." I grabbed the phone and scanned the text.

<< *ED:* 911, 6yo m, nephrolithiasis, lithotripsy >>

"Shit," I muttered, rubbing my temples. "Joey," I called. "Grab your bag. I've got a patient."

He stopped in the hallway. His shoulders drooped. Though he didn't complain or sigh, he trudged to the stairs.

"Quickly," I told him, pushing back my own seat. "It's an emergency." I grabbed my personal phone and shot off a quick text to Noah.

<< *Levi:* Are you home? I just got paged. >>

I shoved my feet into sneakers and grabbed my coat. She texted back as I seized my set of keys from the counter.

<< *Noah:* So much for helping out. >>

I inhaled through my nose. We'd danced this number more times than I could count. It wasn't as if I could ignore pages—especially not emergencies. Not when I was the top pediatric nephrologist in the region. Kids with life-threatening kidney diseases counted on me.

"Joey," I called.

"Coming!" He flew down the stairs, coat half-zipped and beanie askew.

I hurried him out the door and into the Tesla. There was no time to think about how pissed Noah was. Not when a little boy the same age as our son sat curled on a gurney, screaming in pain from kidney stones that needed to be surgically removed.

"I'm really sorry, Joey," I told him as I flew to Noah's apartment.

"It's okay, Dad. I really wanted to go skating."

I glanced at him in the rearview mirror. Sitting in the backseat, he looked so small. "It's just 'Dad' now, huh?"

He eyed me back, challenging me.

"I don't want to cut our weekend short, either," I said. "A little boy just like you needs my help, though."

He nodded. Joey understood because he'd grown up a surgeon's child, but that didn't mean he had to be happy about it.

"How about I pick you up after I get out of surgery?"

"Can we still go skating?"

"If it's not too late, sure."

I pulled into Noah's driveway. She stood by the metal tenants' mailboxes, her arms crossed over her chest, shaking her head at me.

Joey hopped out as soon as I put the car in park. He stood on tiptoes, still not quite high enough to reach the driver's side window. "Bye, Dad."

"I love you, buddy." I cast another glance at Noah.

"Inside," she told Joey softly.

"I'll see you later," I called after him.

She leaned into the window, her face dangerously close to mine. "You can't keep doing this to him," she said in a low voice.

"Babe—" I bit off the word, wincing. Old habits died hard. Taking a deep breath, I continued. "I'm not doing it on purpose, Noah. You of all people should know—"

"Do *not* bring my mother into this," she hissed. "This was your weekend. When are you going to stop making promises you can't keep?"

"Noah." My voice caught on her name. It no longer slipped from my lips with awe. All that remained was regret and longing, with a pinch of annoyance. "You knew who I was when you married me."

"We're not married anymore," she reminded me. "You still have to take responsibility for your son."

"And what? Let someone else's son die in the emergency room? Get my license revoked because you can't handle taking our son on my weekend?" Nostrils flaring, I threw the Tesla into drive. "What if that was Joey on the table? Would you want his doctor to blow off his surgery because his wife—"

"Ex-wife, remember?" She tossed the words at me. "We're done here." She spun on her heel and marched toward the stairs to her apartment.

I eased out of the driveway, wishing it wasn't so narrow so I could peel out. Seething, I headed toward the hospital. Our family was broken, all because Noah couldn't deal with how important my job was.

If only I could've made her see that I'd always come home after surgery. I'd give anything to convince her, except for the one thing I knew she wanted me to give up: my career. I'd find another way.

I had to.

FEBRUARY

❧ 5 ❧

NOAH

The worst thing about New England winters was how they dragged on forever. Even with the sun shining, the earth seemed gray and flat. The cold worked its way into my bones, tangling around my heart. If January seemed long, February stretched into eternity. Growing up, I'd promised myself that I'd move down south, escaping the Connecticut winter. Then I married Levi. Even after our divorce, I couldn't leave the state because of our custody arrangement.

Not that he ever really had Joey.

My days became a monotonous routine: leave Joey with my dad until school started, teach at Watertown High, pick up Joey from school, squeeze in grad school between homework and dinner, work on school work until I couldn't keep my eyes open. Every morning, it began again.

Only my students were excited, crossing off the days on the calendar until the Valentine's Day dance. They buzzed with anticipation. Sighing, I turned from the SMART Board. When I was in high school, teachers still used chalkboards, sometimes whiteboards. Nowadays, we used touch-screen boards that connected to the internet. So much had changed so quickly.

"Let's focus a little, and read out loud from the play." I grabbed my copy of *Romeo and Juliet* and flipped through to where we'd left off.

"Miss Clarke," a girl with a septum piercing complained, "this play is so depressing. Everyone already knows the story. Instead of working to change things for the better, they run away and then kill themselves. Shouldn't we be reading something more inspiring? Like, a *real* love story?"

I parted my lips to tell her to just open her book, but I swallowed my sarcasm. A teaching moment sat right in front of me, and my job was to seize it. I cleared my throat. "So you're telling me, Vanessa, that *Romeo and Juliet* isn't a romance? Which genre would you put it in, then?"

Her partner in crime, Sarah Joy, raised her hand. "Isn't it classic literature?"

"Well, yes—that's where you'd find it in a book store," I said. "Considering the tone and theme, though, which shelf would you put it on if it was published today?"

They stared at me, eyes flat.

"Anyone? Bueller?" I waved the paperback over my head.

"It's a romantic tragedy," a familiar voice rumbled from the door, "and it's tragic that none of you kids know that."

Fighting a smile, I nodded hello to my father. "Romantic tragedy, yes. Does anyone know why we call it that?"

A girl with olive skin and blonde hair raised her hand.

"Yes, Paula?"

"Because the romance doesn't end with a happily ever after," she said. "Like *Romeo and Juliet*."

Relief swept over me. At least one of my students paid attention. I lifted a dry erase marker to the SMART Board, poised to write the key term "romantic tragedy."

The bell rang, cutting off my lesson. "Finish *Romeo and Juliet* tonight and prepare for an in-depth discussion tomorrow," I called as my students grabbed their things and all but ran for the door.

"I see nothing has changed," my father said.

"What are you doing here?" I grabbed my tote bag and a notebook.

"It's Wednesday," he reminded me. "Our lunch date?"

Squeezing my eyes shut, I grimaced. "Sorry. I completely forgot."

"That's okay, kiddo. We can just forget about going for sushi and I can join you in the teachers' lounge." He slung an arm around my shoulders.

"I can't," I said, meeting his blue eyes. Those same eyes and his high cheekbones were reflected in my own face. "I took caf duty."

He removed his arm. "You're on your own with that."

"Gee, thanks."

We strolled out of my classroom and down the hall. Two other teachers had caf duty, so it wasn't a big deal if I was a few minutes late.

"Listen, Noah . . ." Dad paused, running a hand through his salt and pepper hair. "I can't take Joey to school in the morning."

Brows furrowing, I searched his face. He looked the same as always, with crow's feet at his eyes and strands of silver in his dark beard. "What's going on?"

"Nothing," he said. "I just have to go in for a *routine* stress test. Your mother insisted and she scheduled it, and I can't reschedule because the cardiologist is going on vacation. Your mother doesn't trust anyone else." He shoved his hands into his pockets. "You know how she is."

A trio of sophomore boys from my first period class barreled past us.

"No running in the halls!" I shouted.

"Sorry, Miss!" one called over his shoulder as they streaked around the corner.

"Nope, nothing's changed at all," Dad remarked.

"I've gotta go, Dad," I said, forcing a smile so that he didn't feel bad. Panic roiled through my stomach, though. Without Dad, I had no idea how I was going to get Joey to school.

"She didn't do it on purpose." He leaned in and kissed my cheek.

I nodded and we parted ways. A year ago, I wouldn't have worried. Our neighbor would've brought Joey to school if neither Levi or I could do it. That neighbor had passed away around the time I left Levi, though.

If only Levi hadn't insisted Joey go to Stems and Ivy Classical Academy, all the way out in Portland. Then I could put him on the bus like a normal kid, and still be at work on time. There was no way I'd make it all the way out to Portland and back in time. It was an hour away. I'd have to keep him home and call out, bring him in and be late, or bring him with me to work. It might be time to switch Joey to a public school in town.

If I hadn't left Levi, there might be a fourth option.

I parked myself at the teachers' table in the caf, setting my lunch down in front of me but not opening it. I no longer had an appetite.

Molli, my principal's wife and another English teacher, smiled sympathetically. "Kids wear you down today?"

"You could say that," I muttered, pulling my phone out. At least I could escape into the book I'd been reading.

"Mine too." Molli sighed. "I can't wait to get to contemporary fiction, but if their reaction to classic lit is any gauge, I'm doomed."

Nodding, I glanced at my notifications.

One missed call.

From Levi.

The phone vibrated in my hand with an incoming text.

<< *Levi: Call me back.* >>

I lowered my hand. Levi was no longer my husband. He didn't have our child. I didn't owe him a return call. Still, I hadn't really talked to him since our fight a couple weeks earlier. We'd had a few spats in between, mostly because of more of the same. It seemed like every weekend he was supposed to take Joey, something came up.

There was always a patient.

I knew better than anyone else that he saved lives. I just wished he'd make an actual effort. Rearrange his schedule or something. Instead, he jumped at every page, never delegating to the other talented urologists at his hospital.

<< *Levi: Please.* >>

I scowled at the phone.

"Everything okay?" Molli asked.

"Unfortunately," I grumbled. "My ex-husband is alive, well, and driving me crazy."

"That's because he has a penis."

My cheeks flushed. I did *not* want to think about my ex's dick. Thinking about that only led to memories of perfect sex, of nights spent wrapped in his arms. Our marriage certainly hadn't lacked in intimacy—at least, not the physical kind.

My phone vibrated in my hand, Levi's face appearing on the screen along with the caller ID. I probably should've deleted his picture ages ago, but it felt weird to leave his caller pic empty.

"I've got to take this," I told Molli. "Cover for me?"

"Already on it." She smiled, shooing me out of the caf.

I answered just as I got into the quiet hall. "I'm at work, Levi," I said in a near whisper. "What the hell is so important that it couldn't wait?"

"Hello to you, too," he retorted. "I'm between surgeries so I only have a minute, but I wanted to run something by you."

"So run." I rolled my eyes.

"Okay." He hesitated.

"Spit it out, Levi. I'm on caf duty." I wiggled my fingers in hello to the school security guard.

"How would you feel," Levi began, "if I sold the house?"

His words bit into me. "What?"

"The house. Would you be pissed off if I sold it?"

I leaned against a wall. Our house. He wanted to sell the home that Joey lived in for all six years of his life. All of our memories— gone. "It's your house," I said, trying to sound flippant. "You don't need my permission." I sank my teeth into my lower lip. "Why do you want to sell it, though?"

"It's too big," he said. "It's, ah hell, Noah. It's too empty without you and Joey."

"You know," I said, "if you kept him home on your weekends, it wouldn't seem so empty."

"Jesus, Noah. I can't help that, and you know it."

"Whatever." Maybe it was working with teenagers all day, but the word just slipped out. Still, I felt a bit guilty for giving him such a hard time. Plus, I technically had no say in whether he sold or not. I'd given up that right when I walked away. Things were easier that way. "Where will you go?" I asked, voice softening.

"I don't know. I hadn't really thought about it."

Shaking my head, I snorted. Men were so helpless sometimes. "I'll help you look at apartments," I offered. "If you want."

"Yeah? That'd be great, actually." The hope in his voice jerked me back to reality.

I'd just offered to help my ex go apartment hunting.

Nothing about that could go wrong at all.

❦ 6 ❦

LEVI

I paced in front of the three-family home, hands buried in the pockets of my coat to keep them warm. The raw February cold made the memory of January seem warm in comparison. The landlord I was supposed to meet was nowhere in sight, and apparently Noah was running late, too.

My fingers closed around a coin in my pocket, fiddling with it. With the house on the market, and several interested buyers, I'd already packed the majority of my belongings. Thankfully things were moving fast. I just needed a place to live.

A car pulled into the driveway, tires crunching over the packed snow. Out of the corner of my eye, I watched Noah get out. Two seconds later, another car door slammed shut. Small footsteps pounded against the snow.

"Daddy!"

I turned and Joey hurtled into my arms. "Hey, bud. I didn't know you were coming."

Noah shot me an exasperated look over his head. "What'd you think I was going to do with him? Leave him at home?"

"No. It's just a nice surprise." I turned my attention to our son in an attempt to keep the disappointment off my face. I'd hoped to talk to her about the past couple of weekends I'd botched, smooth things over. Those plans were shot, though.

Not that I didn't want to see my son. I hugged Joey again. He was even calling me Daddy again, which had to mean he'd forgiven me. Someday, I hoped he'd even understand.

A boxy old Buick pulled in next to Noah's Camry. My eyes skipped over to the Tesla, which stuck out like a fat lip.

Noah shook her head. "Don't be surprised if he charges you double what he's asking online," she muttered.

"What does that mean?" Joey asked.

Noah glanced at the Tesla. "Nothing, honey."

Joey always caught on fast, though. "Way to be subtle, Dad," he said, eyeing my car.

A short, squat man heaved himself out of the Buick. "Are you my four o'clock?" he asked, glancing from the Camry to the Tesla.

"Yes. Isaac?" I approached him, holding out my hand.

His gaze flicked from the Tesla to me, and he clasped hands with me. "Isaac Berkovits."

"This is *Doctor* Levi Wester," Noah said.

I tossed her a glare. She smiled sweetly.

"I actually have two units available," Isaac said. "I just wasn't sure #1 would be ready in time. We can look at both, and you decide." His accent was an odd mixture of New York Jew and Waterbury Rican. The last name fit the Jewish bill.

Before I could ask where he was from, he gestured to the first-floor unit with one hand, his other hand digging in the pocket of his suit jacket for keys.

"Isn't he cold?" I heard Joey ask Noah.

Isaac led us inside a bright and spacious living room. "All new," he said, pointing to the carpet beneath our feet.

I took a step back toward the door, too aware of my boots caked with sand and salt.

Isaac chuckled. "It's okay. I can just steam clean them again. Come." He gestured toward the rest of the apartment.

"I wanna see my room!" Joey zoomed past us.

"Stick with us, buddy," I called after him.

Isaac waved a hand at me. "Let him. He can't hurt anything."

I glanced at Noah. She shrugged. "I guess it's okay, then," I said, as if Joey had actually come back.

Her eyebrows twitched, but she said nothing.

"Shall we?" Isaac led us further in, lips curled upward.

The scent of freshly dried paint filled my nostrils—one of my favorite smells in the world. Without looking at her behind me, I knew Noah was wrinkling her nose.

I took a deep breath. "Fresh paint."

"Yes sir," Isaac said. He stopped in the kitchen.

"Doesn't it just fill you with possibility?" I asked Noah.

She slid me a flat look. She *hated* the smell.

"All new," Isaac repeated, pointing to the oven and refrigerator.

Crossing the stone-inspired linoleum, Noah opened the oven door and peered inside.

"Clean bill of health?"

Straightening from her crouch, she rolled her eyes. "Central air?" she asked Isaac, inspecting the vent in the floor.

He nodded proudly. "I updated the whole building a few years ago. It's all new."

"Ish," she said. She eyed the vent, considering it. "HVAC is so much more cost efficient," she murmured.

"As opposed to what?" I tried to look alert, as if I knew what the hell they were talking about. Put me in an O.R., and I could perform a laparoscopic nephrectomy in my sleep. Heating and cooling, on the other hand, were a foreign language to me.

"Momma! Daddy!" Joey skidded into the kitchen. "You should see my room. It's got a closet with shelves built into it. I can put all my books in there!"

"Slow down. This isn't a playground," Noah told him sternly. She knelt in front of him. "Remember what we talked about? This might not be your room. Daddy has a few other places to look at."

"Let me show you upstairs," Isaac said.

"I forgot you said there were two units." I gave the first-floor apartment another once-over. It seemed fine. I didn't need much. The price wasn't bad, either, especially for a Watertown apartment. Not that it mattered. I made good money—another facet of my job that Noah had conveniently ignored. We'd been comfortable.

I had to sell the house, though. There was no point in living alone in a four bedroom home—especially not with Noah's memory hanging around the place.

I followed Isaac and my family back outside, then into an exterior door and up a narrow set of stairs. "Either I'm old," I said, "or these stairs are steep."

"Ah, yes," Isaac said with a chuckle. "I won't lie to you—you don't get used to them."

"At least he's honest," Noah muttered. She turned and wandered through the living room and into the kitchen. "Oh," she exclaimed breathlessly.

I charged in after her. "What is it?"

She turned in a circle. "Downstairs has more cabinets. Counter space, too."

"Those are all new as well," Isaac said, following us.

"Momma!" Joey hurtled into the kitchen. "My room up here is even better. It's bigger, and there's a perfect spot for my toy box."

"I guess that narrows down my decision," I joked.

Noah sucked on her lower lip thoughtfully, though. "Are both apartments $850?" she asked Isaac.

"Oh, yes," he said. "Are you looking to rent, too?"

She chuckled. "Ah, no. Not really. Eventually," she added. "The place we're in now is definitely falling apart."

"I do like those shelves in my room downstairs, though," Joey interjected.

"Sorry, bud," I said. "You can't have them both."

Joey glanced from me to Noah. "Why not?" he asked, crossing his arms. He reminded me a little of a stern parent talking to two children.

"Because Daddy doesn't need to rent a whole second apartment, just so you can have two bedrooms." Noah trailed a finger along the marble countertop. "They *are* beautiful apartments, though," she told Isaac.

"Well, why can't *you* buy one?" Joey asked.

I laughed. "Because Momma doesn't need an apartment," I said. "She has one already."

"I do," Noah said slowly, "but these are both so nice." She leaned over the kitchen sink and opened the window. "No death traps when you want fresh air." She chuckled.

"I could open my bedroom window all by myself," Joey added.

Isaac glanced from Noah to Joey, then to me. "You're a family," he said, rubbing his beard like it was a lucky rabbit's foot. "Family should always stick together."

My eyes met Noah's. "If I got paged in for an emergency, Joey could just run upstairs."

Sapphire eyes sparkled. "Oh? You're getting the downstairs apartment?" She put a hand on her hip.

I wanted to tell her that I've always liked it when she's on top, but we had an audience. Besides, I didn't think that would fly anymore. We put on a good front, but we were still divorced.

Living in the same apartment building might not be the best idea. The convenience of it was so tempting, though.

"You could send him *upstairs* when you need to study," I said, already amending my choice. My pulse sped in my veins. I didn't dare to hope, but the idea was too perfect. I'd let her have whatever she wanted, if only we both moved in.

Joey put a hand on each of our hips. "We'd be living together again!" He beamed.

"Well, not together," Noah said. "And we'd have rules. Boundaries."

I nodded. Sleeping at night, knowing she was just a flight below me, might push me over the edge. I knew it might be a terrible idea, but the thought of her so close—even when we were so far apart emotionally—was too tempting to pass up.

Isaac held up a finger. "Shall I go get the applications?"

Glancing up, I found Noah's eyes. "We could help each other out, and we'd both get more time with Joey. What do you think?"

Living together again might break me. Or it'd give me the chance I needed to break down the walls she'd thrown up. I could show her how great a partner I could be. I'd be the husband next door, the guy she'd always dreamed of.

"I'm sick of clogged drains and leaky windows," Noah said. She turned to Isaac. "Let's do this. I'll figure it out as I go."

"Yes!" Joey jumped into the air, pumping a fist. I wished I could do the same. Watching our son celebrate would have to suffice.

Nothing was set in stone yet, though. All I could do was wait, and hope we both got the apartments.

🕊 7 🕊

NOAH

Once the applications were filled out, I had no time to think about what I'd just done because I had to meet my sister. Brynn had never been Levi's biggest fan. She'd called it almost from the moment we met, predicting that he was the type to be married to his job. She'd hate the idea of us moving in together, even if we wouldn't actually be sharing the same apartment.

"Joey." I glanced at my son in the rearview mirror as I pulled up to a red light. "We need a lot of luck to get this apartment. I think we should wait to tell anyone, so we don't jinx ourselves."

"You don't want me to tell Auntie." Joey gave me a look that reminded me of how my dad used to know when I was up to no good but didn't want to call me out on it and get me in trouble with my mother.

"Not just yet, sweetheart."

He looked out the window, and the light turned green.

I moved forward with traffic, absorbed in navigating to Brynn's condo. It wasn't far, but I hadn't been paying attention and I'd taken Main Street. Around rush hour, it was always clogged with traffic as everyone hurried back into town. By the time I pulled into her visitor's parking spot, my stomach growled and my patience was threadbare.

I knocked on the front door, then walked in. "Hi," I called out to my sister. A cool breeze swirled into the townhouse through the open sliding doors that led outside. "I guess the dogs are outside," I told Joey, pulling the door shut.

"Can I go play Minecraft in Auntie's office?"

"Do you mean, 'Can I go look at Auntie's books and pick one to read'? Sure." I smiled brightly at him.

He trudged toward the stairs. He'd probably end up playing Minecraft, anyway, but I'd be happy as long as he read for a little bit. The poor kid. One of the downsides of having an elementary school librarian for an aunt and an English teacher for a mom.

"Brynn?" I called.

"Laundry room," she shouted from the basement.

Sniffing the air, I made my way through the apartment. All I could smell was the intoxicating scent of Gain fabric softener. It didn't smell like she was cooking. I might have to make something, or order in. At twenty-four, my sister wasn't much of a cook.

I joined her in what I called the "half-finished basement." Its walls were insulated and painted a calming blue, and half the flooring was tiled. The other half of the floor was your standard basement concrete.

Brynn stood at a long table, folding small white T-shirts. "Hey," she said. I leaned in and we air kissed cheeks.

"Have you started a laundry service?" I joked, grabbing a shirt and folding it.

"They're for one of my classes. We're a STEM school, so I'm doing a unit on quotes from some books we've read. We're going to tie dye the shirts, then write our favorite quotes on them."

"You are seriously the coolest librarian ever." I bumped my hip into hers.

She shrugged. "I'm just trying to make it work. Don't get me wrong—I love my school. Combining STEM with books is kind of hard, though. There are only so many times we can use the iPads or computers before they get bored."

"Well," I said, "I think you're doing a great job. What's for dinner?"

Brynn laughed. "I figured we could order something."

Stomach rumbling, I set down the folded tee. "Let's get this party started, then."

I trotted up the stairs, Brynn right behind me. In the kitchen, I made a beeline for the drawer where she kept takeout menus. I held up two. "Thai or pizza?"

"That depends. Do you have my nephew with you?"

"I'm in here, Auntie," Joey called from her office.

My sister grinned. "What's your vote, dude?"

"Pizza!"

I slid Brynn a flat look. "Have you learned nothing? He'll choose pizza every time, if you ask him."

She shrugged. "Can't say I blame him."

After calling in our order, we sat in her living room. I claimed a spot on the couch, tucking my legs underneath me.

"So," Brynn said, running a thumb over the pale pink nail polish on her toes, "Mom and Dad's thirtieth anniversary. Do we want a theme?"

Aside from the milestone, my parents' anniversary was a huge deal. They'd stayed together throughout my mother's med school, residency, and years of her putting her patients before my dad, while he stayed home with us girls. Where I'd failed, they'd flourished—though I wasn't so sure about that. Dad had given up a lot to support my mother.

"Well, we can't do anything morgue related," I said.

"That'd be in seriously bad taste." Brynn eyed me. "Any cheerier suggestions?"

My gaze swept the living room, looking for inspiration. Husbandless and childless, Brynn had complete control of how her home looked. Ever since I'd moved out of Levi's house, I'd made it my mission to take back my own space. Where Brynn was all about muted colors like grays, blacks, and whites, I was on a south-western kick.

"They love Lake Tahoe," I said, an idea taking shape. "Why don't we go with a sort of paradise theme?"

"Then we can round it off with a vacation to Tahoe," Brynn agreed.

I snorted. "Right. Even if our mother took off the time, neither of us can afford airfare and accommodations."

She looked down at her lap, shoulders falling. "For a minute there, I completely forgot you were divorced."

"To be clear, you can't stand Levi, but you were totally okay with using his money for things."

"Yes," she said. "How's Joey doing, by the way?"

"He's fine." *He's hoping his parents get the apartments we just applied for—in the same building.* There was no going back, though. I'd just have to let things take their course. Besides, I'd probably get rejected. My credit was terrible without Levi. I waved a hand and forced a smile. "What if we do something more traditional for their party?"

Though Brynn watched me closely, she didn't comment on Joey or Levi any further. "What do you mean?"

"Well, the traditional gift for a thirtieth anniversary is pearls," I said, looking at a list on my phone. *If I hadn't left Levi, we'd be celebrating our seventh anniversary—wool. It was telling that I was allergic to the stuff.*

"Girl, I don't know about you, but I can't afford any pearls."

The doorbell rang and Brynn stood, crossing the living room with her long legs. She pulled open the door and accepted the box of pizza.

"Hi Brynn," the delivery man said, shyness tinging his gravelly voice.

A smile danced on my lips. I couldn't see his face, but I could definitely hear the warmth and familiarity in his words.

"Thanks," she told him. A moment later, she closed the door behind him. "Pizza's here!" she called up the stairs.

I followed her into the kitchen. "He likes you."

Brynn set the pizza down. "So what?"

"So," I drew out the word, "is he hot? He *sounds* hot."

My sister rolled her eyes at me. "You need a life."

"You do, too. He's obviously into you. Why not give him a chance?" I grabbed plates from a cabinet and set them on the table.

"He's a pizza delivery guy."

I put a hand on my hip. "Don't be a snob. What's wrong with delivering pizza? Besides," I added, "it seems like he delivers here pretty often." I wiggled my eyebrows at her.

"There isn't anything wrong with it," she said. "I know him from school. He's the dad of one of my students."

Placing a slice on a plate, I set it down. "Joey! Dinner!" I turned to Brynn. "Is there a rule that you can't date your students' parents?"

"Not explicitly," Brynn said. "We went out for a drink. Once."

"If you worry too much about appearances, you might never be happy." Serving myself, I carried my food into the living room, trying not to think about how it'd look to my family if Levi and I moved into those apartments.

"Appearances are everything, though," my sister said as she followed me. "It wouldn't look good if a teacher dated a student's parent. People would talk."

"You can set boundaries," I insisted. I couldn't tell her about the rules I planned on setting for Levi and me, though—if we even got approved. All I could do was hope those rules would be enough.

Brynn shrugged, as if she could hear my thoughts. "Rules can be broken. And then what?"

And then what?, indeed.

8

LEVI

"Y ou're out of your damn mind," Theo told me, dribbling
the ball toward the hoop.

"Maybe," I said, darting in front of him and stealing
the ball, "but I've gotta try." I ran toward the other end of the
court. He'd take it back in no time, but for the moment I had the
upper hand—and it felt pretty fucking awesome. When your best
friend is a professional basketball player and a giant, you've got to
take small victories when you can.

Pun intended.

Just as I went for a layup, Theo reached out a long arm and
batted the ball away. My feet hit the ground and I turned from the
court, shaking my head.

"Come on. You really thought you could beat me? They pay me
the big bucks to win." He joined me at the sidelines where we'd
left our things against the chain link fence.

Theo and I were the only ones on the basketball court in the
middle of February. I wrestled my bottle of Gatorade out of the
snow pile I'd buried it in, then handed him one.

"It keeps me in shape, so I can't complain," I said. As a

surgeon, staying fit helped me spend long hours in the O.R. It also helped me show my patients that even though there were a lot of things they couldn't do, they could still be active.

"Right." Theo poured half the bottle into his mouth, then wiped his face with the sleeve of his Under Armour shirt. "I still think you're nuts. Noah left your ass. How are you going to get her back?"

"First, we have to get those apartments." I hadn't thought about the rest of it. Leaning against the fence, I stared at the empty, frozen park. In the spring and summer, the place hardly ever sat empty. In winter, though, it looked like a ghost town.

Theo clapped me on the shoulder. "You know I've got your back, dude, but this seems like a long shot."

"It is," I agreed, "but I have to try."

He nodded. "I respect that." Finishing off his Gatorade, he tossed the bottle into a nearby garbage can. Then he frowned. "You're not the only one trying."

"What do you mean?" I mopped sweat off my face with a towel, then retrieved my keys. Wordlessly, we headed toward the parking lot. Though the silence between us thickened with each step, it wasn't uncomfortable. It was the space between thoughts, a moment of reflection.

As we neared our cars, Theo stopped. "I'm retiring," he said.

"So soon?" I joked.

"I've waited as long as I can, but they told me it's time. I've aged out." Shoulders rising and falling into a slump, he ambled toward his SUV.

"Shit, I'm sorry, man. What are you going to do now?"

"That's the problem," Theo admitted. "I don't know—and Pamela wants to start a family. It's a lot."

"Yeah." Shoving my hands into my pockets, I headed toward the Tesla. "If all else fails, I can get you a job at the hospital."

He slid into the driver's seat. "Really? Like a surgical assistant?"

"I don't think they let basketball superstars play with scalpels.

It'd be something like housekeeping or food." Climbing into my own car, I started her up and turned the heat up to high. We weren't moving around anymore, and the cold bit through my Under Armour gear.

"All right, man. I 'preciate it. I'll see you later." Theo closed his door. A second later, he backed out of his spot and drove away.

I sat with the engine idling, watching the SUV fade from view. Life was so short—anything could come whipping out at you around the corner. It was more important than ever that I convinced Noah that we belonged together.

◈◈◈

JOEY SAT ON THE COUCH, LEGS STRAIGHT OUT IN FRONT OF HIM. He balanced a textbook and notebook on his lap.

"Whatcha doing, Joey kangaroo?" I asked, sitting next to him.

Brown eyes flicked my way, then returned to the book in front of him. "Reading."

I glanced down. The anatomy of the human heart spread across the page. He'd roughly sketched the diagram in his notebook. Not bad for a little kid. "This isn't your book from school." Pride swelled in my chest.

"It's your book," he said.

"I know it is." I tapped my fingers on my thigh, thinking.

"I'm sorry." Joey clapped the book shut and pushed it off his lap. His eyes rounded as he silently begged me.

"I have to tell Mom," I said after a moment. His lower lip trembled at my words. "Not because you're in trouble," I added. "I mean, I wish you would've just asked instead of taking it. Some of my books are a little . . . advanced for you."

Hell, all of my medical books should've been beyond his six years. Yet there we sat, my son studying cardiac anatomy—on his own. Noah was going to freak. Whether she liked it or not, though, medicine was in his blood, from both sides of the family.

"I'm not in trouble?" he asked.

"No, buddy." I booped his nose. "I'm really proud of you right now. Are you interested in being a doctor? Like me and your Nan?"

"Will I make Momma sad?"

Swallowing surprise, I picked up the book and notebook and set them on the coffee table. "Why would you ask that, kiddo?"

"Nan makes her sad, and so do you. If I become a doctor, I'll make her sad, too."

I cleared my throat. Not for the first time, my own son had me stumped. Most six-year-olds were curious. It was typical for their age. Joey, on the other hand, picked up on more than most children his age. I didn't know how to explain to him that his grandmother hadn't been very warm to his mom when she was little. With Noah for a mother, Joey probably couldn't wrap his head around something like that. Besides, I didn't want to spoil his view of his Nan.

"Momma's not sad because Nan and I are doctors," I said, picking my way carefully around the subject. "She's sad because . . ." My voice trailed off as realization slammed into me.

Throughout the entire nine years of our marriage, Noah had relived her childhood. Instead of a mother who was never around, though, she'd been stuck with a husband who wasn't. It wasn't that she couldn't understand why I had to go when I got paged—she knew that better than anyone else. Every time I walked out that door, though, I reminded her of all the times her mother walked out on her.

I hadn't meant to be distant, but I took my work home with me—even when I wasn't working on a particularly difficult case. That phone was always on, always by my side. Every time it rang, it took me away from her.

From our family.

"Daddy?" Joey's anxious eyes searched mine.

"Your Momma misses your Nan, buddy," I said, voice thick. "That's all."

"Does she miss you too?"

"I don't know." But I was going to find out. "Come on, Dr. Joey. We're late for dinner at your Grammy's."

Even as an adult, I still wasn't used to my parents being divorced, living apart. As I drove us to my mother's, I wondered if it would ever feel normal to Joey, or if he'd find himself a grown man, wishing his dad was coming to dinner too.

I didn't want to find out the answer to that particular question.

I'd accepted a long time ago that my father was gone. In his place, I vowed to build my own family. Somehow, I'd find a way to prove to Noah that I was sticking around. I wouldn't leave her—ever. She'd never feel abandoned again, for as long as I lived, if she only gave me a second chance.

Opening the door to my mom's small house, I ushered Joey inside. After my parents split, my mom went back to her maiden name, bought herself a house in Farmington, and grew her thriving gift basket business. Around town, she was known for making people a cup of tea when they walked into her little store on Route 6. Even though it was a state route with four lanes of heavy traffic, my mom's store had a small town feel.

Without my father, my mom was thriving.

I hoped Noah didn't feel so light without me around.

"My boys!" My mom bustled into the living room. Joey threw himself into her arms and she gave him a kiss on the cheek, leaving behind a smudge of red lipstick. Mellie Campbell was *that* grandma.

Adjusting her teal cat eye glasses, she turned to me. "You look too skinny," she admonished, wrapping me in a hug.

She ushered us into her eat-in kitchen, where dinner waited: pork roast, potatoes, green beans, and salad. All of my favorite things.

"Sit, sit," she said, waving us into chairs.

"This is quite a spread," I told her. "What's the occasion?"

"Can't I just celebrate my boys coming for dinner?" she asked.

If Noah and I got back together, I'd celebrate every moment— even mundane ones like doing dishes after dinner.

I smiled back at my mom. If Noah and I got those apartments, I could easily see us having family dinners. That was my plan: give her and Joey my all and make us a family again, and hope every-thing else fell into place.

✤ 9 ✤

NOAH

Two weeks passed before I heard anything about the apartment, and by then I knew I didn't get it. My credit score was tanked between my maxed-out credit card and past due electricity bill. As far as I knew, Levi hadn't heard back, either.

I sat at the kitchen table, its surface covered in notebooks and printed out articles. The cursor blinked on the screen of my laptop, waiting for me to start writing my paper.

I opened up Firefox instead.

Typing in the address, I hunted for the apartment. It was still listed. Maybe neither of us got it, and the landlord decided to keep looking. He'd turned down a surgeon, though. I could understand him passing over a teacher, but Levi had a steady income. No way was that hospital ever letting him go anywhere.

Levi excelled in med school so much that hospitals were practically fighting over him when he finished his residency. He took the position at Yale even though other offers were even better.

"Yale is the dream," he'd said. "I can't ditch the dream."

Levi and I had very different opinions of New Haven.

It was the place I avoided. Between the traffic clogging the

47

streets, the eternal road work, and the random people strolling across the streets, even with oncoming traffic both ways, I had no patience for the place.

My ex loved New Haven, even though we'd gone to university in Storrs. He was the guy who drove all the way out to Pepe's just for a slice of pizza.

In his years at Yale, Levi made it his goal to try every restaurant in the city. Before and after Joey was born, we spent countless nights driving around, Levi scouting, assessing. Circling back through one-way streets didn't bother him. Not while he was on the chase. Meanwhile, I always scarfed down a stale granola bar, fighting the urge to hop out of the car and run for the nearest McDonald's.

My eyes returned to the empty document on my screen. I was supposed to write a strategic plan for myself. The more I thought about mission and vision statements, though, the more I wondered whether I was completely in over my head.

I didn't know the first thing about being an author. All I knew was that I loved to read, and that I'd spent years building up contacts as a book blogger. I had the connections and the audience. I just needed my own books.

Picking a single genre and sticking to it was hard, though. I didn't consider myself a romance author—no matter how much I secretly enjoyed Hallmark movies or how many times I played matchmaker to characters on TV shows. I wanted to be known as a storyteller.

First, though, I needed a story. A series, preferably—to prove to readers that I was in it for the long haul. Before I could start writing, though, I needed to pick a genre.

Rubbing my temples, I closed my laptop. The strategic plan would have to wait.

The screen of my phone lit up as it rang silently. The caller ID flashed a number that I didn't recognize. Usually I let those go to voicemail—they were usually bill collectors—but the number was from Watertown.

"Hello?"

"The woman of the hour! How are you?"

"Good?" My uncertainty made the word a question. "Who's this?"

"Ah! My apologies. Isaac Berkovits. You came to see two of my apartments a couple of weeks ago."

"I remember you," I told him. My heart fluttered. Prospective landlords only called for two reasons: to get more information, or to tell you that you got the place. No one ever called to tell you that you didn't get it.

"You can arrange to move in on the first of March!" His smile reached me through the phone.

I grinned so big, my face hurt. "Really?"

"Really. Of course, I'll need a deposit beforehand: first month, last month, and security. It'll come to . . ." Papers rustled in the background. "$2,550," he said.

My face fell. Even with my savings, there was no way I could swing that up front. I couldn't borrow any more money from my teacher's credit union, either, and I sure as hell wasn't going to ask Levi for help. I could ask my parents, but that really meant asking my mother. "Well, thank you Isaac, but I'm going to have to decline."

He shuffled some more papers. "I'll tell you what. For you, I'll just take first month's rent and a security deposit of $500. How's that?"

I glanced at the refrigerator that threatened to quit any day. My current landlord refused to replace it, instead having someone fix it every time it stopped working. The window in the bathroom leaked, and the kitchen sink faucet was corroded from the hard water, its washers stripped.

Joey and I needed something more reliable. Plus, if his dad got the other apartment, Joey would see more of both of us.

"Isaac," I asked slowly, "may I ask if Levi got the other apartment?"

"I can refuse him if you two aren't getting along."

"Oh, no, no. I'm just making sure we both got them."

"I see. You know," he said, "you two are the most amicable divorced people I've ever met."

Ha, I thought. *You should've seen us the other day*. Once again, Levi had to bring Joey back to my place early—in the middle of the freakin' night. If we lived in the same building, I could just go upstairs and sleep on the couch when Levi got paged in for an emergency. Joey would sleep soundly, never missing his daddy.

"Yes," Isaac said.

It took me a moment to realize he'd answered my question. "Great," I said. "When do you want to meet for the deposit?"

"Can you both come by this evening?"

I glanced at the time. Levi had a rare day off and had picked up Joey from school. We were both free. I set a time with Isaac and hung up, my stomach doing slow flips.

An amicable divorce. There was no such thing. Levi and I just kept it friendly for Joey's sake. Moving in together was going to require me to keep it more than just friendly. We'd be co-parenting, no excuses. There was no denying that it was the best thing for Joey, though.

I just wasn't sure if it was the best thing for me.

❧

I PULLED INTO THE DRIVEWAY NEXT TO LEVI'S TESLA, SHAKING my head at it. Unlike at the house we'd shared, his car was out of place in our new neighborhood. I sat back in my Camry, fingers loosely wrapped around the steering wheel. I was *really* going to walk into that first floor apartment and sign papers, once again intertwining my life with his.

The lease only lasted for twelve months, though. A year. I could do a year.

Before I talked myself out of it, I shut off the engine and climbed out into the cold. By the time we moved in, spring would be on its way, stubborn winter still vying for control of the region.

I could put potted flowers out in front. Joey could even have a kiddie pool in the summer. There was plenty of room in the yard.

We could even put out some patio furniture.

Correction: *I* could put out patio furniture. There was no "we" anymore.

Taking a deep breath, I held my head high and knocked on the door to the first floor apartment. Then I nudged the door open, hesitating on the threshold. Technically it was my place. I could just walk in.

"Come, come," Isaac beckoned me from inside, his voice echoing in the empty space.

Following his voice, I joined him in the kitchen. I smiled, suddenly timid. 14 Edgewood Road, Apartment 1 would be the second place I'd ever rented on my own. I'd gone from living with my parents to sharing a dorm room with Pamela to living in an off-campus apartment with Levi. Then came our house, after Levi became a resident surgeon at Yale.

The place I thought would be our forever home.

"I'll be right back," Isaac called as he left the room. "I forgot something in the car." A moment later, the front door closed behind him.

Levi leaned against the refrigerator, his ankles crossed and his arms folded.

"Are you sure you want to sell the house?" I blurted.

"I'm sure," he said, voice low. Dark brown eyes burned into me, simmering with what looked like determination. That couldn't be, though. He already had the apartment. We both had what we wanted. Unless he'd changed his mind about taking the third floor.

I glanced around. "Where's Joey?"

"Helping his Grammy make a big pot of sauce and meatballs." Levi pushed off from the fridge and crossed the room toward me. The way his eyes never left mine sent my blood singing through my veins.

I swallowed. "How is Mellie?" I stammered.

"She's good," he said, voice still a low rumble. He stopped only inches away from me. "I'm glad we're doing this." His tone was hushed, appreciative.

I turned away. "We should probably come up with some ground rules." Crossing the room, I hopped up onto a counter, safely out of his reach. Having him in my space brought the past rushing back, causing my body to fall into muscle memory. Even on the counter, my body still leaned toward him, yearning to lock itself into his arms.

I couldn't let that happen.

"Ground rules?" Levi's brow furrowed. "Like what?"

"Like boundaries," I said, mouth quirking.

"Boundaries?"

"We need to respect each other's spaces." I fixed him with a pointed look.

He held up his hands and stepped back. "Of course. What else?"

"What do you mean, 'What else'?"

"I still know you, Noah," he said softly. "There's always more." Those eyes latched onto mine again, snapping up my heart and tugging it out of the depths I'd locked it in.

My gaze dropped to my hands, severing the connection. "No romantic partners sleeping over."

"That won't be a problem."

"I mean it, Levi." I looked up, avoiding his eyes. I settled for the bridge of his nose. "If we're seeing anyone, we have to use hotel rooms if we want to be . . . intimate." Drawing a breath, I met his eyes. He frowned back at me.

I sighed in exasperation. If we couldn't agree on even basic things, there was no way we'd be able to occupy the same building for the next year.

"That won't be a problem," Levi explained, closing the distance between us.

"What's that supposed to mean?"

❧ 10 ❧

LEVI

For me, it was simple. There was no one else in heaven or on Earth who I wanted more than I longed for Noah. Obeying her rule would be easy, because it was already part of my plan.

"Because I don't plan on being intimate with anyone else," I said, placing my hands on the counter and caging her in. Every kitchen we'd ever christened came rushing back at me in a heady slam.

"Levi," Noah said on a sigh. Her fingers skimmed up my arms, ghosting over my biceps and lighting on my shoulders.

"I don't want anyone else," I continued, leaning into her. "Let me prove to you that I can be the man you need."

Placing a palm on my chest, she gripped a handful of my shirt and crushed it into a ball in her hand. "Levi," she said again, tugging me close.

"Yeah?" Blood surged through my veins, charging up into my head and down, making my jeans tight. Just being around Noah intoxicated me. Being alone with her drove me crazy. I couldn't remember the last time we'd been unaccompanied, in the same space at the same time.

"This 'ship has sailed," she said firmly, pushing me away.

The front door opened and I staggered back.

"You two kids behaving in here?" Isaac strolled into the kitchen, a gleam in his eye.

Cheeks flushing a fierce pink, Noah hopped off the counter. "Let's just get this done." She plucked a pen from the counter. "Where do I sign?"

"Hold your horses," Isaac said, producing a folder and flipping it open. He slid a packet toward Noah, then held one out to me. "You should read your leases."

I stood at the other end of the counter, holding a pen between my middle finger and thumb, bouncing the pen back and forth in the air like a metronome. As I leaned over the lease and pretended to read, a strand of hair fell into my eyes.

I'd just tried to kiss my ex-wife.

Instead of meeting me halfway, she'd rejected me—hard. My plan to woo her was never going to work if I kept letting my body do all the talking. If I was going to get her back, I needed to put out the fire burning inside me and stay cool.

Around her, though, I could barely think.

"All done?" Isaac cut into my thoughts.

I hadn't read a word of the lease. Straightening, I pointed the pen at him. "I'm going to need a copy of this."

"That *is* your copy." He eyed me as if he could read every thought churning in my skull. Then he handed us each another copy. "This is mine. We each sign both."

"Great," Noah said. "Who do I make the check out to?"

"For what, my dear?" Isaac asked, cocking his head to the side.

I bent over the leases, scrawling my signature. Just like everyone always said about doctors, my handwriting and Hancock were terrible. I eyed the print on the sheets so hard they might've burst into flames, and silently willed Isaac not to give me away.

"For the deposit and first month," Noah said, as if he were old and forgetful.

"Oh." He chuckled. "That. Don't worry about that."

"What do you mean?" She placed her pen on the counter. "We have an agreement. I thought."

I chanced a glance at her. Eyebrows knitted, she searched Isaac's face.

"You're all set, my dear," Isaac said. Coming out of his mouth, the pet names didn't sound creepy. He reminded me more of a kindly grandpa, especially with the tweed yarmulke he wore.

Noah crossed her arms. "What do you mean," she asked slowly, "I'm 'all set'?"

Though he said nothing, Isaac glanced my way.

Her arms fell to her sides with an audible clap as her hands slapped her thighs. She wheeled around on me. "Are you kidding me? I don't need your money!"

"It wasn't supposed to be my money." I scowled at Isaac. "He was supposed to tell you he'd decided to give you a break."

Noah's hands balled into fists. "Levi Wester, you are unbelievable, do you know that?"

Involuntarily, the corners of my mouth twitched upward. "Unbelievable, huh?"

As her own memory was triggered, Noah's fists relaxed. Her lips trembled as she searched for words. My smirk widened.

"You're blushing, Noah constrictor."

Her cheeks blazed a deeper shade of red. "That," she stuttered, "is *not* appropriate."

Isaac cleared his throat. "While I'm sure at least two-thirds of us are enjoying this awkward moment, I have some errands I need to run. If you would," he said, gesturing to the papers.

Blinking, Noah shook herself out of the memory. She handed Isaac his copy of the lease. "We're not done here," she told me.

"I'm counting on that." I passed my papers to Isaac without taking my eyes off her.

"Your keys." Isaac passed keys around. "There are two sets of each, if you want to give each other a copy." With that, he bustled out, an amused look on his face.

Noah and I circled each other in the kitchen.

"You can't just rush in and pay for my apartment," she said, the anger gone from her voice.

"Our son is living there. It's my responsibility." Her lips parted to argue, but I held up a finger. "You can pay me back later," I said, knowing full well that I'd refuse her.

Still, it appeased her for the moment. "Fine. Are we done here?"

"Never," I said, voice low.

She swallowed, a lump rising then falling in her slender throat. I thought of all the times I'd trailed kisses across the soft pale skin there, and my cock immediately went hard.

Again.

"What else?" Her tone matched my own, as if we'd stepped into a church together.

"We still have to go over the ground rules."

"Boundaries and hotels—those were really the only ones," she said. "I just don't think Joey needs to see us coming and going with other people. He's . . . still adjusting."

I locked gazes with her, studying those triangular eyes. We both knew that Joey had been doing better. He didn't completely understand, and he obviously wanted his parents back together, but neither I nor his pediatrician would describe him as "adjusting." Not anymore. He'd finally adjusted. His innate intuition made him a resilient kid.

Sometimes, it was as if he knew something we didn't.

"Well," I said, "it's either celibacy for me . . . or you."

She shook her head. "I guess you'll be a monk, then." She grabbed her purse from the counter. "I've got to get back to my homework."

"Wait." I stretched out a hand as if I could pull her back to me. As if time and years of hurt hadn't physically and emotionally separated us. I took a deep breath. "I have one more condition."

She rolled her eyes. "If you're suggesting neither of us date, period, you don't have to worry about me. I don't have time for that." She looked pointedly at the digital display on the stove.

"That's good to know," I said, "but this is something else. I'm hiring a housekeeper for us."

Noah snorted. "A housekeeper? Is this a joke? It's the twenty-first century. I'm more than capable of doing my own laundry."

"Of course you are. I'm not hiring her because I don't think you can handle it. I'm hiring her because I know *I* can't, and I know you could use the free time. Any extra time we have is time that Joey gets."

Time that I got with her, too, but I didn't mention that.

Her lips parted, and I heard her sharp intake of breath from across the room. My shoulders tightened. I'd tried to do something nice for her, and I'd screwed it up. Twice.

"Okay," she said on an exhale.

"Really?"

"Yes." She pointed a finger at me. "But I'm still doing my own cleaning. I just can't justify making another human being clean up after me."

"It's a deal." I held out my hand.

She glanced down, teeth sinking into her plump lower lip. "I think it's for the best if we just make this a verbal agreement." Gathering her things, she headed toward the front door. As she walked into the cold evening, she called a goodbye over her shoulder.

I remained in the kitchen, watching her go, a smile on my lips. She didn't want to touch me. She'd felt what I'd felt, before Isaac walked in. She didn't know it yet, but we were meant to be together.

And I was going to do whatever it took to convince her.

MARCH

❧ 11 ❧

NOAH

I stood in front of the floor-length mirror, the one I'd dragged with me from my parents' house to my college dorm to my old place. The reflection staring back at me lifted an exasperated eyebrow, disapproving of me moving in with my ex.

I didn't disagree with her.

"No turning back now," I muttered, smoothing the long-sleeved UConn alumni tee I'd chosen for the day. It was threadbare and in danger of gaining a hole, but I liked the way it flowed around my hips. Also, it didn't hurt that it'd seen better days. If anything happened to it while I was schlepping boxes and furniture between apartments, it wouldn't kill me.

Nor would I be upset about the leggings I wore, their knees shredded from a few years earlier when the hobo look had been in fashion. I hung onto them for banging around the house—or singlehandedly moving.

Luckily, I had reinforcements.

Knuckles rapped on the door, punctuating my thoughts. Pamela strolled in. "Hey, baby!" A few seconds later, she rounded the door frame to my bedroom. "Look at you."

"Me? Look at you!"

Despite it being the first day of March and one step closer to spring, New England weather had other plans. The drizzle outside wasn't ice, but it was close enough.

Pamela spun in her T-shirt dress and rain boots, her outfit more appropriate for early fall. "You like it?"

"I think you're going to be cold."

She wrapped her knee-length cardigan tighter around her. "Not with this on. I've discovered that T-shirt dresses are like wearing sweats, except it looks like you tried *and* you don't have to put on pants."

"Whatever you say." I shrugged. "Where's Theo?"

"Directing the movers into your driveway. I always knew it was tight, but I can't imagine trying to back a fifteen-foot truck up this bitch."

"Truck? I didn't order a truck, Pamela. My dad is coming with his pickup." Brushing past her, I ran to the front window. Sure enough, a professional movers' truck was backing up my narrow driveway. "What the hell?"

Pamela joined me at the window, bumping her shoulder against mine. "I think it's sweet. Don't you?"

It had Levi written all over it.

"I'm going to kill him," I said under my breath. Raising my voice, I called out to Joey. "Are you dressed, Joe-a-roni?"

"Ready, Momma," he said, emerging. He wore the beanie, corduroy pants, and I MAKE SIX LOOK GOOD shirt I'd laid out for him the night before.

At least one of the men in my life respected my wishes.

"You're leaving in—" I grabbed my phone, scrolling through my texts. "—ten minutes." While Pamela, Theo, and I loaded the pickup, my dad would take my car and drop Joey off with my mother.

"I hope Tibby lets me look at her medical books," he said.

"Since when do you call your Nan by her first name?" Eyebrows furrowed, I fired off a text to Levi. Too much was going on at once.

"She asked me to," Joey replied, turning back toward his room.

"Of course she did," I muttered, waiting for Levi to text me back. My phone *ding*ed and vibrated in my hands, making me nearly drop it.

<< **Noah:** *Your truck is blocking my dad from getting into my driveway.* >>

<< **Levi:** *You're welcome.* >>

Ellipses appeared as he typed another response.

"I'm going to kill him," I said to Pamela again. "Look at this." I shoved my phone in her face.

"Jeez, woman. I'm not near-sighted!" She pushed my hand away to a more legible distance. "I really think he's just trying to help."

"He can help by *not* helping. Would it have killed him to ask what my plans were before sending me . . . ?!" My voice trailed off as movement in the driveway caught my eye. Four men in coveralls emerged from the truck. "Movers," I finished, my brain catching up.

"Still pissed?" Pamela's eyes glinted.

I shot her a look, then headed toward my front door to wave them inside. It wouldn't hurt to have a few more hands. As the movers traipsed up the stairs, my phone went off again.

<< **Levi:** *I didn't want your dad to hurt his back trying to help.* >>

I pressed my lips together. It certainly was thoughtful of him. It was also forward in an obnoxious way. It was weird enough that we were moving into the same house. Unless I'd hallucinated the whole thing, we *had* talked about boundaries just a couple weeks earlier.

<< **Noah:** *Next time, please check in with me first.* >>

I didn't have any cash to tip the movers, nor had I planned on feeding an extra four mouths after we were done. Still, it eased my mind. I wouldn't put it past my dad to try to help, anyway. With the movers on the clock, he had no excuse to jump in.

<< **Levi:** *I'm counting on there being a next time.* >>

I read the text again. *What the hell does that mean?* My brow wrinkled. I didn't have time to figure it out, though. The movers marched into my apartment, barely giving me a nod as they passed me. They traipsed to my dining set, yelling to each other in mover talk.

"This last?"

"Couch first!"

"Stack 'em, stack 'em!"

I ushered Joey out of the way as the guys began wrapping his bed in heavy blue moving pads. They looked like thick quilts, the kind that you'd put between your sheets and a comforter during winter—if you run cold like me. The scent of grease and aftershave wafted to me, though, shattering the illusion.

My phone pinged again, Dad letting me know he'd arrived.

<< **Dad:** *I thought we were using my truck.* >>

Sighing, I led Joey downstairs.

"Pop!" Joey ran down the last flight while I grimaced, waiting for him to take a spill, scrape a knee. He didn't, though, his feet as sure as a surgeon's hands. He flung himself into my dad's arms, Dad lifting him up high.

He'd always been fit.

As I came down the last few steps, I caught the tail end of their conversation.

"Your Nan got called into a surgery," Dad explained to Joey. "It's just you and me today, Jay-Jay!"

Not even the sweet nickname could curb the flash of anger

63

that ripped through me. My mother and Levi—they were one and the same. I couldn't count on them for anything, and neither could Joey.

That, in a nutshell, was why I'd left.

Both of them.

"Hop on in," my dad told Joey.

He skipped along to the passenger's side of the truck, then climbed in. Sitting in the cab, my little boy looked even smaller. He waved, and I waved back.

Dad hugged me with one arm, the scent of his cologne enveloping me for a moment, cool, clean, and sure. "How are you doing, kiddo?"

"He was excited to see her." I crossed my arms.

"I know," he said, stroking his salt and pepper beard. "He's got me, though, and if he sleeps over, he'll see her in the morning." Triangular blue eyes studied me, pleading.

"Okay, 'Pop,'" I conceded. "I'm sure Joey will be thrilled."

He ducked his head, but not before I saw the wide grin on his face. "So what's up with the truck?" he asked, gesturing to the thing hulking in my driveway.

It was a good thing we were moving *out*, because my soon-to-be ex-neighbors were about to hate me.

"Levi," I said with an exasperated huff. "He thought it'd be easier if he hired movers."

Dad tucked his hands into the pockets of his thick zip-up hoodie. "Well," he said, toeing a chunk of snow with his white classic high-top Reeboks. "I guess I'll take Joey out for lunch, then."

"I really appreciate it," I told him, standing on the balls of my feet to plant a kiss on his cheek.

"I know, sweetheart. It's probably better for my back, anyway. Give me a shout if you need me," he said as he got into his truck.

I waved as they drove away, then took a deep breath. Without the excuse of our son, there was nothing to distract me once Levi and I occupied the same space. I had Pamela and Theo, but those two were Switzerland.

I was on my own, and that terrified me. With a whole town between us, I'd *almost* been able to forget how much I loved him. It wouldn't take long for me to remember.

Not long at all.

My heart was about to be tested.

❧ 12 ❧

LEVI

I paced the length of my still-empty living room, trying to stay out of the movers' way as they carried furniture and boxes into my bedroom. So far, I hadn't heard a truck pull up. Either Noah had turned them away even after our texts, or something had gone wrong. I was about to pull out my phone and call her when the rumble of the truck's engine roared onto our street.

I made myself walk to the window.

Sure enough, Noah stood next to the truck, arms gesturing as she directed the movers. I grinned, unable to help myself. Even if she was annoyed with me, I'd saved her a day of sore muscles. I pulled out my phone.

<< **Levi:** *Now you can just get in there and unpack as they bring things in.* >>

My grin widened.

It was really happening.

On the street, Noah reached for her phone in her car. I couldn't see her face. Her head ducked, reading the text. The sleek ponytail she'd pulled her hair into trailed over one shoulder. She wore that ratty UConn shirt that I simultaneously loved and hated.

Loved because it reminded me of the days when everything between us was as new as that shirt. Better days, when I snuck into her dorm room and Pamela snuck into mine to be with Theo.

Hated, because seeing it on her reminded me of what I'd lost. No more peeling that shirt off her, my mouth covering hers as she laughed, Joey sleeping soundly down the hall.

She looked up at the window I stood at. It might've been my imagination, but I swore our eyes locked for a second.

<< *Levi: I'll be right down. Don't move.* >>

Before she could answer, I jogged down the stairs. They were narrow and steep, a testament to the house's age. Not at all like the home we'd shared, where everything was less than a decade old. Throughout college, med school, and then my residency, my dream had been to build her the home of *her* dreams. My salary as a resident wasn't that impressive, though, and with Joey on the way, we'd needed something fast. That house hadn't been what our hearts desired, and without her it was too empty. I wasn't sad to see it go.

I couldn't wait to make new memories with her.

I slowed as I reached street level. I wanted to appear cool, despite the near tachycardic pulse racing beneath my sternum. I pushed the door open and strolled over to her.

"Hey," I said as casually as I could muster.

She took in my navy blue henley and dark gray joggers. "Day off?" she asked, an eyebrow raised.

"Hopefully," I joked. "If I have to leave, I might come home to my kitchen table in the bathroom."

"They're not *that* bad," she said, efficiently killing my joke.

I shrugged, not deterred. After all, I'd just completed the first phase of winning her back. Instead of lugging furniture around, she stood outside chatting with me. That alone was a victory, but I'd only wanted to make her day easier.

A small victory in a long and difficult journey. She was worth every step, though, no matter how many blisters formed on my heart.

"How did Joe take the news?" I asked, referring to her father.

"Surprisingly well." She crossed her arms, shivering in the late winter wind. "I kind of expected him to try to help the movers, but he actually took Joey to lunch."

"Good." I tried not to look too much at the shirt—to avoid tracing the slope of her shoulders, the contours of her arms, the swell of her breasts, and the outline of her bra beneath the thin fabric. I swallowed. "This shouldn't take long."

She cast a sideways look at me. "No. I suppose not."

"I figured I'd order a pizza," I blurted. "You know. After. Would you like to join me?" I gave her wide eyes, knowing she'd probably see right through me anyway.

Noah sighed. "I've got chicken salad in a cooler. Wait!" Turning away, she hurried after a pair of movers carrying what looked like her curio cabinet wrapped in moving pads. "That was my grand-mother's. *Please* be careful with it."

They won't break your heirloom, I wanted to tell her. It was my job to break things that were precious to her.

With our conversation seemingly over, I turned and trudged back upstairs behind a mover carrying a box. He set it down on the kitchen counter and went right back down to the truck filled with my belongings. Crossing the apartment, I went into the kitchen, stopping at the box. One of the movers had labeled it KITCHEN, not bothering to get more specific than that.

I couldn't bear packing up what little of our history I had left, so I had the movers do it all for me. When people got divorced, they typically threw their ex's things away. Burned pictures. That sort of thing. Not me.

When people got divorced, they were supposed to part ways without looking back. Neither of us had been able to do that, and I didn't think it was just because of Joey. There was too much between us, too much history. Pieces of our story that couldn't be left heaped on a tag sale table—or worse, in a garbage collection pile.

The fact that Noah was speaking civilly to me without Joey around was testament to that. She didn't have to give me the time of day, yet she didn't seem to be able to ignore the pull between us any more than I could. It was only a matter of time.

I just needed to be patient.

I had one more card up my sleeve, though. I withdrew my phone from my sweats and texted Theo.

<< **Levi:** *Are you guys staying after we're done? I'm gonna order pizza.* >>

Then, using my keys, I sliced open the tape that held the box closed.

❧

THE FOUR OF US SAT ON THE FLOOR OF MY LIVING ROOM, SLICES of pizza in our hands, bottles of beer open on the coffee table. It felt good, sitting there with Noah and our friends. Like old times.

At first, when I told Noah that Pamela and Theo were going to stay, she'd sent me an emoji rolling its eyes. When I sent her a pizza emoji, the greater than sign, and chicken and salad emoji next to each other, she conceded.

She'd never been able to say no to me for long.

I couldn't tell her yet how much I still loved her, but in the meantime I could shower her with pizza with extra pepperoni. She'd grown up in Watertown and, even when we were at UConn, never stopped talking about Martino's pizza, so that's what I'd ordered. Noah was my past, present, and future—and I planned on showing her that in whatever language she'd accept at the time.

"We should play Cards Against Humanity," Pamela said, setting down her slice onto a paper plate. She reached for her purse.

"Oh no." Noah held up her hands, a fingertip covered in sauce.

Before the divorce, I would've grabbed her hand, taking that finger into my mouth and sucking on it. Then I would've pulled her into my lap, pressing my mouth to hers, my cock hard against her warm center.

"That game is trouble," Noah continued.

Someone knocked at my door, interrupting the debate. I glanced at the time on my DVR box. Right on schedule.

"Perfect timing," I said, jumping up. I opened the door wide. "Come on in."

The woman I'd hired to be our housekeeper strolled in as if she owned the place. Her eyes scanned the room, scrutinizing every surface.

"Alice," I said, "meet my friends Pamela and Theo, and my . . . Noah." I cleared my throat, hoping no one noticed my near slip. "Everyone, this is Alice—our housekeeper." My eyes met Noah's.

I'd chosen Alice because of her no bullshit personality, but also in part because she was no threat to my and Noah's relationship. With her graying dark hair, olive skin, and curved, wide mouth, Alice was stunning—even more so with the crow's feet at the corner's of her warm brown eyes. However, she was devoted to her wife of forty years, their five children, and dozen grandchildren. She was the best surgical nurse I'd ever had the pleasure of working with, and a font of advice and humor.

"Hello, hello," Alice said in greeting. She smiled, and it lit the room. "I'm just going to start some laundry and do some vacuuming in here and downstairs. Those movers clearly don't know how to wipe their feet." She eyed the dirt tracked across the unfortunate white carpet. "Then I'll be back in the morning after I get the twins off to school." She headed into my bedroom.

Theo lifted his eyebrows at me, impressed. "Well played," he mouthed over Noah's head.

"I think I like her already," Noah said.

Phase two was under way.

❧ 13 ❧

NOAH

Stretching, I stood from where our group clustered on the floor, stifling a yawn. With Joey at my parents' for the night, I could afford to stay up a little. I'd overdone it, though, and needed to get up early if I was going to get any school work done before he got home.

Not to mention the unholy amount of unpacking that lay in my future.

"I've got to call it a night, guys." I carried my disposable plate and cup into the kitchen. Somehow Levi already had most of the room set up. I ran my fingers along the kitchen table that had once been ours. I touched its finish, worn and scratched from spilled nail polish remover and a few times when toddler Joey got hold of a pen.

Levi could've replaced it. I'd bought a new dining set almost immediately after leaving him. He certainly had the money for it, and Joey was old enough to treat a new table well. Yet there our old table stood. He'd held onto it for no reason.

Unless there *was* a reason.

I couldn't go there, though. Not if my heart was going to make it out alive and beating.

"I'm glad we can do this," Levi said, his voice soft in the dark kitchen.

I tossed my plate and cup into the garbage can, and turned to face him. "I don't really know that we're *doing* anything."

He leaned on the wall, arms loosely crossed, one ankle hooked over the other. "We're having a game night with our friends."

"Just a last-minute one," I reminded him. "This won't be a regular thing."

"Won't it?" Pushing off the wall, he closed the distance between us. "We're neighbors now, Noah."

Two inches taller than me, Levi had always fit snugly with my body. I didn't dare lift my chin. He stood close enough to kiss me, and every single nerve within my body seemed aware of that tiny fact. Or maybe it was bigger than that. I raised my eyes to meet his, and almost gasped when I read what lay in those open depths.

He wanted to kiss me.

I swallowed, laying a palm on his chest. Heat radiated from him, and his heart thumped underneath my touch. I'd intended to push him away. My hand remained on him, though. I couldn't pull away. Or maybe my hand still remembered how to linger, even when my mind knew I shouldn't.

"Noah," he whispered. His voice caressed me, sending warm tingles dancing along my spine, the back of my neck, across my scalp. Lifting a hand, he ever so gently tucked a strand of hair behind my ear. He'd always loved when my ponytails got a little messy.

My eyes fluttered closed while my brain screamed at me. I shouldn't let him kiss me, but that part of me had lost control from the moment he walked into the room.

Maybe even earlier.

Just that tiny action sent my senses into overdrive. I wanted his hands doing more than just brushing my hair away. I wanted them on my skin, a thumb on my nipple, his lips on mine—

The kitchen light flicked on.

I jumped back from him, turning away as if he'd burned me.

"Whoops," Pamela said, slinking into the kitchen. "Sorry."

"Thank you," I mouthed to her.

She shot me a disappointed look as she threw Theo's and her garbage away. I couldn't tell whether she was upset that I'd almost kissed him or annoyed with herself for interrupting.

"We're gonna get going, too," she said.

Levi cleared his throat. "Yeah. I guess we should call it a night."

"Goodnight," I called over my shoulder. I tried not to look like I was running away, but I couldn't help it. I grabbed my phone and booked for the door. As I descended the narrow stairs, I heard voices behind me, but shook them off. It sounded as if Pamela was chastising Levi.

In the safety of my own apartment, I kicked off my sneakers and socks and padded around barefoot. It was bigger than my last place. The bedrooms were farther apart, and the couch and desk in the living room were less cramped.

The freshly vacuumed carpet squished under my toes as I scurried across it like a little kid. I'd always loved the softness of carpet after being vacuumed, and Alice had used some kind of freshener too. The whole place smelled like clean laundry.

The thought reminded me that I needed to make at least my bed so that I could crash after showering. Alice mentioned doing some laundry, so I checked the closeted washer and dryer first.

Empty.

She must've washed and dried my sheets, then made up the bed for me. I was beginning to like the idea of a housekeeper.

I made my way into my bedroom, flipping on the light as I entered. I took in my bare dresser, missing its knick-knacks. I'd have to unpack them another day. A wall of boxes sat in the corner, also waiting their turn. The closet sat open, some of my clothing already hung. The rest wouldn't wrinkle in their boxes, so that could wait too.

My gaze lighted on my bed.

My very *naked* bed.

Frowning, I glanced around for the box marked SHEETS. Alice

must've decided not to do laundry after all. It wouldn't kill me to sleep on sheets that smelled like cardboard and packing tape. I'd washed them before folding them and packing them away, anyway.

Spotting the box, I climbed toward it. As I reached for it, though, I already knew.

The box had already been opened. All of my sheets were gone.

I closed my eyes and took a deep breath. Maybe Alice hadn't realized that I had a washer and dryer. Maybe she'd taken everything to a laundromat. Or she'd washed everything upstairs, in Levi's laundry closet.

The last thing I wanted to do was go back up there, but I couldn't sleep on a naked mattress. It was weird. If the zombie apocalypse ever came, and I had to sleep on bare mattresses to survive, I'd be the first one to go.

I needed amenities like sheets and hot water, damn it.

Fuck it, I decided. I'd just take a quick shower and sleep on the couch. I had plenty of throw blankets. When I went into the bathroom and turned on the hot water knob in the shower, though, nothing came out.

The throw blankets box had been opened, and they were gone, too.

Scowling, I shoved my feet into slippers and marched back outside and up the stairs to Levi's. Pamela's car was gone, but the lights in the apartment still shone through the windows, so I knocked.

Loudly.

Levi opened the door, brow furrowed. As he realized who it was, though, his whole face lit up. I pushed past him into the living room.

"Your housekeeper," I seethed as he closed the door behind me, "took all of my stuff. And somehow I have no hot water. I have no water, period!"

He blinked. As my words sank in, he frowned. "What's missing?" He grabbed his phone. "I'll call the police."

"My sheets, my blankets—all of my linens!" I sputtered.

He set his phone down, but his brow furrowed deeper. "Why would she do that?"

"How the hell should I know? I *thought* she was doing laundry." I jabbed a finger in the air at him, taking a step closer.

"Alice is good people," he said, eyebrows still knitted. "She works at the hospital. I've known her for years. She and her wife certainly don't need sheets."

"This isn't funny."

He held up his hands. "I'm not mocking you. I'm just confused."

"Shocker," I said.

"Hey." He gently took my shoulders. "I don't know what's going on, but we'll figure it out."

His eyes held mine. They'd always captivated me, their shade not quite brown but not quite green or gray, either. An almost amber hue lit them from within. I used to think it was the color of his soul. He wasn't supposed to be the good guy in my story, though. He'd been the one to hurt me, and I'd become my own hero.

Still, I couldn't tear myself away. His touch was light but the heat from his hands poured into me as if I was thawing after a long winter. Lips parting, I tried to tell myself that he should let go of me.

Nothing came out, though.

The heat in his eyes and hands spread through me, consuming. Without breaking eye contact, he leaned forward, closing the inches between us. I watched his lips near mine and braced myself for impact.

It never came.

Levi's phone chirped and whirred on the coffee table. He snapped back, blinking as if clearing a daze. I knew the feeling.

He crossed the room and picked it up, a groan escaping his lips as he read it. Tipping his head back, he closed his eyes. "I have to go," he told the ceiling.

Relief swept through me, quickly dampened by disappointment. I turned toward the door, feigning indifference. "I need to get to bed anyway," I said.

"Wait." He put his phone down and darted into my path to the door. "Sleep here. My bed is made. I'll just crash at the hospital, or on the couch." Holding his hands up as if I were a deer he might startle away, he grabbed his keys. "Just . . . stay." Without another word, he opened the door and disappeared into the night.

"Sure," I told the empty living room. "No problem."

I stood there, hesitating. I was tired to my marrow, though. Something about moving always energized me, but by the end of the day I was spent. Sinking into a freshly made bed appealed to me in the way that a cheeseburger after going days without eating appealed to me.

"Besides," I said with a sigh, "he'll probably sleep in an on-call room, anyway."

Clicking the deadbolt into place, I turned from the living room. Joey's bedroom door stood open, his bed and toys already arranged. Most of his belongings were downstairs, with me. For a moment, I considered sleeping in my son's bed. The twin mattress was small, though, and I'd always been one of those sleepers who spread out. Having a whole bed to myself had been one of the perks of divorce.

If splitting your life into pieces had any.

I'd made the right decision, though, I reminded myself as I turned toward the closed bedroom. Levi's room.

The weight that had pulled on my neck and shoulders disappeared the moment those divorce papers were signed, my life back in my own hands. I no longer had to live by the vibration of an incoming page. Except when Levi dropped Joey off early.

Or when he took off in the middle of a near kiss.

I pressed the pads of my fingers to my lips. We'd been so close, his mouth only inches from mine. Kissing Levi would not only be playing with fire—it'd be soaking myself in gasoline and dropping a lit match on my foot. Because even a year after separating, the most visceral part of me wanted him.

Which meant he still had a piece of my heart.

I shouldn't be sleeping in his apartment, never mind in his bed. I shook my head. I'd just grab the comforter from his room and make Joey's bed work. Or I could even take it upstairs, where I could put a lock between us.

Nodding in resolve, I turned the knob and pushed the door open. It took a moment for my eyes to adjust to the dark. I knew those curves anywhere, though: the polished wooden globes atop the posts, the filigree sweeping across the headboard and foot of the bed, the wood stained dark and varnished to a shine.

Levi still had our old bed.

❧ 14 ❧

LEVI

I slipped my key into the lock, turning it and pushing the door
open as quietly as I could. Outside, the first tinges of pink
touched the sky as the sun rose. I didn't want to wake Noah
—if she was even still in my apartment.

I moved through the dark living room with my hands stretched
out. Somewhere, I had light bulbs for the lamps, but I hadn't
unpacked them yet. Things like that were Noah's domain when we
were married. I was still working out my own system.

My shin slammed into a piece of unseen furniture, demon-
strating how well my "system" worked for me. I gritted my teeth,
trapping the string of swears I'd unleash on the thing if Noah
wasn't sleeping on my couch. I made my way to my bedroom as
best I could. A blue nightlight glowed in Joey's room, but it didn't
reach past the door.

Maybe I needed my own nightlight.

I found my own door and pushed it open. I'd thought about
staying at the hospital, but my patient was stable. Besides, the
possibility of waking up to coffee with Noah, just like old times,
was enough to convince me to haul my ass home.

Kicking off my sneakers, I stripped out of my scrubs. I'd never been so glad to sleep in my own bed. Though I had plenty of stamina for long surgeries, the shorter emergency ones always drained me—especially since I became a father. There was something gutting about having a small person on my table. Even when they pulled through, the surge of adrenaline always wore me out.

I climbed into bed, automatically reaching for the pillow I usually slept with. Instead of a pillow, though, my hand closed around a soft mound. I patted the area, fingertips grazing soft skin.

Noah.

She moaned in her sleep, curling into me. I froze, heart thumping in my throat. Every molecule in me wanted to wrap my arms around her, to bury my nose in her hair and inhale her as I slept. She wasn't mine anymore, though. If I had any hope of getting her back, I had to tread carefully.

I peeled my arm away slowly. She rolled over, nudging me to the edge of the bed. Curling into my ribcage, she rested an arm on my chest, her hand over my heart—muscle memory. On its own, my hand closed over hers. Our bodies always remembered, even long after our hearts tried to bury the past.

"Levi," she whispered, my name a sigh on her lips.

I could've remained just like that for the rest of the night. I wanted to. I didn't have the right anymore, though. Shifting beneath her, I tried to untangle our entwined bodies. I patted around for another pillow, something to replace my body.

"Levi?"

I froze. Silence stretched over us. After a few beats, I figured she'd only stirred in her sleep. I hadn't woken her. When I resumed inching off the bed, though, she clutched my bare chest with her hand.

"Wait."

In the dark, I couldn't see whether her eyes were open. She'd always talked in her sleep. For all I knew, she was dreaming of better days. Sometimes I dreamed of those days, too. Taking her hand, I gently tugged at her arm so I could slide out.

She wouldn't budge.

"Noah," I whispered on a sigh. Either I could wake her up, or I could just deal until the morning. It couldn't be much longer 'til her alarm went off, according to the amplifying pink in the sky. She had to be up for my mom to drop off Joey. It wouldn't kill me to stay put.

She might kill me, though.

In the end, I wasn't comfortable with remaining in the position we were in—both literally and figuratively. No matter how good it felt to have her arms around me, I knew that in the waking world, she'd sleep on the floor before sharing a bed with me. Heart twisting, I returned to the task at hand: getting her hands off me. Her delicate fingers might as well have been super-glued to me, though. They stuck to me as if her life depended on it.

I shook her arm. "Noah," I called. "Let go-a." The late hours were catching up to me.

She stirred, warm body shifting against mine. Her arm moved, hand exploring my chest. Her fingers reached my face, tracing my lips.

I pried her off. "Wake up, Noah. Please."

With a gasp and a jerk, she wrenched her hand away. Sitting up, she scooted to the other side of the bed. "What the *fuck*, Levi?"

I stood and crossed the room, switching on the light. "It's not what you think," I said, grabbing my scrub pants from the floor and stepping into them.

"Oh, really?" She crossed her arms. "What is it, then?"

"I thought you were on the couch."

"You *told* me to sleep in the bed." She glared at me.

Even with her hair in sleepy waves, her clothing rumpled, just looking at her made my chest ache. "I'm sorry," I told her, voice thick with not only fatigue, but also emotion.

Getting her back was the only thing I wanted in the whole world.

"Did I . . . ?" She motioned to my side of the bed.

I could've ribbed her for it, but the naked vulnerability in her eyes doused any urges to tease her. I sat on the bed. "You, you know, cuddled up with me."

"Oh." She looked down at her hands in her lap. "Like we used to before?"

"Yes." I swallowed the thick lump in my throat, shoving the old feelings down. I'd only been kidding myself. It was over. We were no longer Levi and Noah. There was just me, and just her.

Shaking her head, she kept her eyes on her hands. "I guess seeing the bed just kind of sent me back through a time warp."

"Right," I said, fighting to keep my voice light. "Makes sense."

"It just surprised me, you know?" She took a deep breath, stormy eyes pinning me. "I didn't think you'd still have it."

Shrugging, I looked away. My eyes drew right back to her as if magnetized. "Just haven't had time to go furniture shopping."

"Of course." She lifted a hand. "Makes sense."

I frowned. I couldn't tell if she was being sarcastic or not. My eyes felt swollen and gritty in my head. "I need coffee." I stood, bolting for the door, eyes down. She collided into me, our bodies jumping back from each other as if we'd been burnt.

"Sorry," she said.

Seconds ticked past as my heart thudded in my throat. All I wanted to do was tell her I loved her. How much I missed her. That I needed her. "I got an espresso machine," I said instead.

"Oh? That's good," she said, voice soft and hesitant.

I gestured to the door. "You can, uh . . ." My voice trailed off.

"Sure." Glancing at me quickly, she darted past me.

Squeezing my eyes shut, I tipped my head back and clutched at my sternum as if I could reach in and hold the pieces of my heart together. I couldn't, though, so instead I followed her into the kitchen.

"Alice should be here soon," I told Noah as I focused on getting the machine going. "We can find out what she did with your sheets. Then I'll call Isaac and find out what's going on with your water."

"You don't have to do that." She circled the kitchen, fingers ghosting over where the items should've been labeled on boxes. "Any idea where the movers packed your espresso cups?"

I rubbed at the back of my head. Whoever packed the kitchen had merely checked off the room on the box, not bothering to go into detail. "Your guess is as good as mine." I joined her at the stack, wordlessly handing her a butter knife.

The room became noisy at the espresso machine heated up and knives slid through tape. We ripped open boxes, tossing packing paper onto the floor.

"Glasses," Noah called out.

I joined her at her box and peered inside. "These are just the plastic cups, for Joey." I drummed my fingers on a box flap.

We both saw it at the same time, the only unopened box. Even though I saw her go for it, I moved toward it too. Our hands met as we both reached for it.

"You do the honors," I said, staring into those eyes.

We stood frozen, hands still touching. She turned toward me, lips parting, her head starting to shake. A lock of hair fell into her eyes. Slowly, I reached for it, brushing it out of her face.

Maybe it was the lack of sleep catching up to me. Maybe it was the way she looked at me, like a deer in headlights. Or maybe it was the memory of her hand on my chest, my name on her lips as we lay in my bed.

Dipping my head, I tilted her chin up. Then I pressed my lips to hers.

At first, I just brushed my mouth against hers, testing the waters. Her trembling lips moved against mine as her hand grazed the stubble on my cheek. Noah buried her fingers in my hair, the familiar move shifting something inside of me. Putting a hand on her hip, I drew her closer to me, the lines of our bodies blurring.

Then she stepped away. "The bed," she exclaimed. "It's just the bed." Turning, she ran out of the kitchen, back downstairs before I could say another word.

APRIL

❧ 15 ❧

NOAH

Holding a hot cup of vanilla chai in my hands, I leaned against the counter of my new-to-me kitchen. Any minute, Alice would be knocking on my door with a fresh load of laundry. We'd have a few moments alone to talk. The chai should've steadied my nerves but my hands shook. I set the mug down.

"Hello," she called through the door as she lightly tapped her knuckles against it.

Pushing off from the counter, I moved through the kitchen, then the living room. As I unlocked and opened the door, I took a deep breath. "Hello," I said.

She stood holding a laundry basket full of towels and blankets. "I'm so sorry about the other night. I put away Levi's linens but somehow yours came home with me." She held the basket out to me, her silver hair glinting in the morning light. "I don't even know where my mind was." She chuckled.

"Thanks," I said, taking the basket and shifting it onto my hip. "Alice . . ." I hesitated. "I appreciate what you and Levi are doing." We had a housekeeper before, when Joey was just a baby and the mountains of tiny laundry seemed unimportant compared to snuggling my new son. "I think I can handle my own laundry, though."

Her brown eyes studied me from behind green cat eye glasses. "I'm sure you can," she said. "I'm just here to help."

I licked my lips. "Alice, do you know anything about my hot water heater?"

Her forehead creased. "No, dear, I'm afraid I don't."

"Are you sure? Because my landlord says it's brand new and should be fine, but I've had to take showers . . . upstairs." I sighed. As if sleeping in my ex-husband's bed hadn't been mortifying enough, Joey and I had to use his bathroom, too. At least until Isaac sent someone out to take a look. Thankfully, Levi was rarely home.

A glint of amusement flashed in her eyes. She clapped her hands together. "I'll tell you, dear, I've never met anyone like your husband."

"Ex-husband," I corrected.

"Levi is a good man. You should have him take a look at your water heater—of which I truly know nothing about. I did take your linens home, though." She smiled sweetly.

The woman was old enough to be my mother. In another life, she could've been. How much warmer my childhood would've been if I'd been raised by someone like her.

My phone vibrated in the back pocket of my jeans. Fishing it out, I read the text that flashed across the display.

>> *Mom: Your father just informed me you moved. Are you out of your mind?* <<

Grimacing, I locked the phone and tucked it back into my pocket. "Alice, I know Levi adores you, but I'd really appreciate if you'd stop meddling with things. Thank you for the laundry." I smiled, hoping it showed my appreciation for her—without encouraging any more matchmaking games.

"Oh, it's no trouble," she said. Flashing me one more smile that I swear held a hint of mischief, she turned and left.

◈❧◈

COLD SPRING RAIN LASHED THE WINDOWS, OFFICIALLY welcoming New England into April. More like hazing, actually, but we were lucky it wasn't still snowing. I sat crosslegged in bed, my laptop balanced on my knees. Since moving in, I hadn't touched my work in progress, and I'd fallen behind on my grad school work. Every week left me struggling to catch up. Thankfully, spring break was coming. I'd get one blessed week off from both work and school, and I planned on using it to finish my book.

And finish unpacking.

The gloom surrounded me as I scrolled through the course discussion board. If I didn't get a post up before midnight, I'd lose points. With how distracted I'd been, I couldn't afford the loss. The school would kick me out if my GPA fell below 3.0.

Levi's face floated into my mind, his kiss from that first night burning on my lips. Even with a whole floor separating us, I felt him. I'd distanced myself from him, communicating only out of necessity. As if summoned, my phone buzzed, his name flashing on the screen with an incoming text.

<< **Levi:** *Do you mind if Joey stays up here tonight?* >>

On his rare day off—he was usually on call—he wanted to spend time with his son. Of course I didn't mind. There would be no emergency pages, no dashing out the door. I sent him a quick reply, then switched off my ringer. I needed to get some work done.

I couldn't focus, though.

Every night I stared into the darkness, feeling my heart beating, wondering what would've happened if I'd kissed him back. If

I'd stayed. I lay in my bed while he lay in ours, our hearts tethered despite the stairs between us. I missed him.

The truth might as well have been written across my palms. There was no going back, though. No matter how much of an effort he was making with Joey, there was too much pain between the two of us.

Sighing, I set my laptop aside and hopped out of bed. I walked through the gloomy apartment, turning on lights as I moved into the kitchen. A whole pot of beef stew simmered in my Crockpot, and I had no idea how I was going to eat all of it. I could invite Pamela and Theo over. As much as I wanted to see my best friend, though, I had a lot of work to get done. I couldn't afford the down time.

The house ticked around me, the antique clock in the living room echoing all throughout the apartment. Since it was bigger than my old place, the empty spaces seemed that much bigger when Joey was gone. I stirred the beef stew, inhaling the savory scent of cooked meat and veggies in broth.

There had to be a way I could get myself back to zero—even with Levi upstairs. Even during the week, when I had a routine to lean on, he infiltrated my every thought.

My phone buzzed in my pocket. Putting the Crockpot lid back on, I snapped its buckles into place. Then I fished my phone out.

<< **Levi:** *Something smells good. What's cooking?* >>

I blinked. I couldn't remember a single time throughout all six years we'd been married that he'd complimented my food. He wasn't around enough.

I knew I shouldn't even respond to him. Even though I wasn't angry about the kiss and didn't exactly have a reason to give him the silent treatment, I needed to reinforce the boundaries we'd discussed. Maybe it was because I so badly wanted living under the same roof to work, but I'd gone out of my way to get along with him that first night. I'd let him sway me with pizza and games, but it needed to stop.

Joey needed parents who could cooperate—he didn't need us to be friends. I started to slip my phone back into my pocket when the GIF came through.

Jensen Ackles chewing.

I bit my lip in a feeble attempt to stop my smile. Levi knew me too well, and he'd exploited my weakness. "Damn it," I muttered. Damn *him*.

<< ***Noah:*** *Beef stew.* >>

I added a GIF of Jensen Ackles playing his guitar leg, because I'm a rockstar when it comes to beef stew. Not that Levi knew that.

A second later, Jensen Ackles in a lab coat and scrubs appeared on the screen, the GIF captioned with "Hi" as Ackles's lips moved. I could watch those lips all day.

<< ***Levi:*** *Beef stew sounds way better than pizza.* >>

I snorted. The man was using my obsession as a weapon against me, and it was working. I sent him Ackles smirking.

<< ***Noah:*** *Send Joey down. I'll send some up.* >>

A few seconds later, I heard my son's little elephant feet running down the stairs. He darted through the living room, bursting into the kitchen.

"I'm Flash!" He struck a running pose.

"Oh?" I ladled stew into a plastic container. "Is that what you're watching?"

"Yeah," he said, his big brown eyes bright with excitement. "Daddy and I are on episode four." He launched into a recap of the series so far while I snapped a lid on the stew and rummaged for a paper bag for him to carry it in.

I pictured the two of them cuddled on Levi's couch, and smiled. With us under the same roof, Levi was no longer a weekend dad or, in some cases, a two-hour dad. Joey could spend time with him whenever he wanted. My own hangups didn't matter, not with my son getting what he needed.

I handed him the bag. "Okay, Barry Allen. Two hands. No running."

He started to give me the stink eye, then tilted his head. "How do *you* know who Barry Allen is?"

"Oh, kid," I said, shaking my head. "I'm just as cool as Daddy is—if not cooler. I'll show you all of my *The Flash* comics this weekend."

Eyes round as saucers, Joey gaped at me as if I'd just told him I was Wonder Woman. "Cool," he breathed. Then, blinking himself out of his awed trance, he sprang to the balls of his feet. "Text Daddy and tell him I'll see him in six seconds!"

"Even The Flash can get burned," I reminded him. "That's hot."

"Daddy has his doctor kit," he said. Still, he walked to the front door and, even though his feet were still loud on the steps, he walked upstairs.

At his age, I'd thought my mother was a superhero, that I could never really get hurt because she was a doctor. Doctors fixed people. They didn't break their hearts. Maybe Levi wouldn't break Joey's heart like my mother broke mine.

In a few months, I'd be throwing her an anniversary party like everything was just fine between us.

Twenty minutes later, as I sat at my laptop at the kitchen table, my phone lit up with an incoming text.

<< **Levi:** *This is really good. Thank you.* >>

Underneath his words, Jensen Ackles gave me a thumbs up.

I wished Levi could suture the cracks in my heart closed.

⚭

I SLEPT BETTER THAT NIGHT THAN I HAD IN A WHILE. MAYBE IT was the beef stew, or that I'd finally caught up on school work. I woke up to a text from Pamela.

> << **Pamela:** *Theo says your little cub is with Levi. We're going shopping, Mama Bear!* >>

Rubbing sleep out of my eyes, I sent her a thumbs up emoji. We hadn't gone shopping together for something that wasn't groceries in years—never mind on a Sunday.

Shopping with Pamela was always a marathon event. We'd be running all over the place, so I needed to wear something comfy and warm. I dressed quickly in black leggings, shoved my feet into gray UGGs, and reached into my dresser drawer for a long-sleeved shirt. I pulled out a muted red henley, the kind that Joey always called a waffle shirt.

It was Levi's.

I ran my fingers over the thermal material. I used to steal Levi's thermals all the time, usually to sleep in but sometimes to run errands in. Glancing around guiltily, I brought it to my face and inhaled. The clean scent of Gain fabric softener filled my nostrils. Underneath it, though, I could still smell Levi's cologne, its crisp, woodsy scent intoxicating.

Alice must've mixed our things up when she last did laundry. It turned out that she was an excellent housekeeper. Sometimes, though, she made odd mistakes. Like accidentally taking my sheets home with her that first night. Or leaving my vacuum upstairs at Levi's, even though he had his own.

I sniffed Levi's shirt again. I'd have to talk to Alice myself. I was starting to think she was doing it all on purpose. She was his co-worker, after all.

A horn beeped outside and I jumped as if I'd been caught. I pulled the shirt on over my head quickly, threw a beanie on over my wavy hair, and grabbed my North Face coat. I didn't give a shit how "basic" I looked. I was warm and it hadn't taken a hundred layers like in *A Christmas Story*.

I slid into Pamela's car, already reveling in her heated seats.

She handed me a hot latte. "Morning, bitch." Despite the cool April morning, she wore a T-shirt dress and thigh-high boots with socks that peeked up over them.

"Are you conditioning yourself for Alaska? Jesus." I sipped the latte gratefully. Just looking at her made me shiver. So much for being warm.

Pamela narrowed her eyes, her gaze zeroed in on my chest. "Oh. My. God. Are you wearing one of Levi's shirts? Did you two sleep together?"

I zipped up my jacket. "Has Theo found a job yet?"

"Touché," she said, pulling out of my driveway.

His shirt caressed my skin, and I wished that it was his hands on me instead.

❦ 16 ❦

LEVI

Every so often, I got a case that required me to stay at the hospital for several days. Noah never liked those. As I shoved clothing into a duffel bag with Joey by my side, I finally saw why.

"So you're going to work to play dominoes?" he asked with a frown.

Laughing, I sat next to him. "I'm not playing dominoes, buddy. I'm doing a domino surgery."

His brow only wrinkled further.

"It's a surgery where a big group of people all pay it forward. Each patient gives another patient one of their kidneys."

Joey's face scrunched as he tried to understand.

My boy was smart, but he was still only six. I needed to break it down to his level. "You know how on your birthday Momma sends cupcakes into school with you? And you share all of your cupcakes with your classmates?"

He tilted his head at me, both confusion and frustration in his eyes.

"Then, when it's the next kid's birthday, he brings in cupcakes for everyone, too," I continued. "It's like that."

"Everyone only has two kidneys, though," Joey said, as if I were the kid and he the doctor.

"Right—"

"So you're giving away both your kidneys? You're going to die?"

"No, nobody's dying." I lifted him onto my lap, wrapping my arms around him. Kissing his forehead, I inhaled his scent. It'd been years since he smelled like a baby, but Noah always swore that she could pick him out of a lineup by smell alone. She was right. Joey's hair was a mix of sunshine and the pages of old books, with a hint of sweat thrown in for good measure.

"What are you doing?" Jerking his head away, he twisted until we were eye to eye.

"Nothing, bud," I said with a sigh. "I'm not giving away either of my kidneys. I'm coordinating the swap."

He stared at the wall thoughtfully for a moment. Then he faced me again. "Like a bake swap?"

"Exactly like that, Banjo Joey."

He tossed me a glare that still managed to be adorable. "Don't call me that. I'm not three—"

Scooping him into my arms, I stood and strode to the center of the bedroom. I held him with one arm while my free hand hovered above his belly, the threat of an imminent tickle attack. "Banjo Joey!" I bellowed as he giggled, then tickled his belly and ribs as if he were a banjo.

Or guitar, at this point.

He was getting so big.

He howled with laughter, suddenly my three-year-old boy again. As I tickled him, I made what Noah used to call horrible banjo sounds: "Bow bow bah bew bow!" Somewhere on YouTube, there was a video of me playing Banjo Joey that'd gone somewhat viral.

Joey had gotten a lot heavier since then. I lowered him onto the bed and sat next to him. His squeals died. Slowly he sat up on his knees. "Do you really have to go?"

Up until then, I'd never had to have this conversation with him.

It'd always been Noah. Swallowing, I turned to face him. "I do. It's my responsibility."

"What about your priorities?" he asked. In that moment, he looked and sounded so much like Noah, my chest tightened.

"My priority," I said, standing again, "is keeping you in a good school. You know, taking care of you and your mom." Stuffing the last bit of clothing inside the duffel bag, I zipped it up.

My son's round eyes tracked my movements. "I can go to public school," he offered.

That was new. Joey loved his school. Part of the reason we'd picked his private school was because he was so advanced. I'd gone there, too, and yeah, I felt a certain pride, like maybe he'd be a doctor someday, too. All I wanted, though, was for him to get a good education.

"You know," I said, looking him in the eye, "if you went to a public school here in town, you wouldn't have STEM again until middle school."

He frowned.

"Where's this coming from, buddy? I thought you liked Stems and Ivy."

Shrugging, he traced the piping on my duffel bag. "I want you and Momma to be married again," he mumbled.

I glanced at the alarm clock on my nightstand. I needed to leave, or I was going to be late. An entire team of surgeons relied on me to lead them through the procedure—never mind the patients, donors, and their families. I didn't want to just leave without talking, though. My shoulders sagged with all of the weight. "Joey—"

"I know, I know. You have to go, *Dad*." He slid down from the bed and trotted out of the room. A second later, I heard him stomping down the stairs toward Noah's apartment.

"Shit," I muttered. There was no time, though. I shot a text to Noah as I gathered my things and ran down to the Tesla.

>> *Levi: Can you please tell Joey we're not done talking?*
>>

Her response came in as I pulled out of the driveway: a single question mark. Then my phone went off again.

<< *Noah: What the hell did you say to him?* >>

With one hand on the wheel, I ran the other through my hair. There was never enough time. Never enough words. Using the voice-to-text feature, I fired off a response.

<< *Levi: He wanted to know why we can't get married again.* >>

Maybe it was immature of me, but I was sick of being the bad guy. She'd left me, not the other way around. She could handle our son's questions.

No other texts came in.

I pulled into the hospital staff parking lot, sliding into a space. Grabbing my things, I climbed out, adrenaline soaring. Not just because of Joey, either. Like any surgeon, I was a junkie.

The bag bounced against my thigh as I raced to the surgical floor. I silenced my phone, shoving it into my scrubs pocket as I changed. I left my overnight bag in my cubby, firing off a reminder to an intern to claim a bed for me. As ready as I could be, I turned, nearly bumping into the Chief of Surgery.

"You ready for this, Dr. Wester?" he asked, eyeing me. Unlike on *Grey's Anatomy*, the medical world was still run by old white men. Dr. Combies was an excellent surgeon, but the guy was a total dick.

"Of course, sir." I regarded him coolly. "Are you going to watch?"

"Of course, *doctor*," he said, his voice measured and chilled. It reminded me a bit of how my six-year-old called me "Dad" when he was angry with me.

We scrubbed in together in silence. Each scrape of the bar soap against my skin washed away my problems, stripping everything away until I was just a surgeon. In the O.R., nothing else mattered. It was just my hands and my brain working in tandem together, cutting away problems and stitching everything back together neatly.

If only it were that simple outside the hospital.

⚜

THE SIX-WAY DOMINO KIDNEY TRANSPLANT TOOK ABOUT TEN hours the first time it was done at Johns Hopkins in 2008. My team did it in eight hours.

"Is there a Guinness record for this?" my scrub nurse, Octavia, asked as we scrubbed out. "Because if there is, I'm pretty sure we broke it." She did a little victory dance, her deep brown hands dripping suds onto the floor.

"Watch that ego," I said, chuckling.

"Dr. Wester, if I were you right now, I'd have the biggest ego anyone had ever laid eyes on." She shook her head at me and resumed scrubbing.

"Will having an ego make a difference when I suggest you get some rest?" I asked, nodding to her very pregnant belly.

"Nope." She popped the P. "Not unless you're suddenly my doctor or husband."

"How is Niall, by the way?" I finished drying my hands and we headed out of the unit. Every muscle in my body ached. I needed at least six hours of sleep, but 6:00 a.m. rounds were in less than four. "How's YouTube treating him?"

"Good." Octavia trundled beside me, her nearly black curls bouncing as we walked. "YouTube Red ordered a pilot from him, so he's actually in L.A., shooting it now. If they like it, they'll order a ten-episode first season."

"Ten, huh? Seems like a short season." We came to a T junction in the hall. One way led to the caf, the other to an on call room.

"I guess they do it that way so they don't take such a big risk on you." She shrugged. "Niall says if those episodes do well, they'll order more. He's written several versions of his first season, all depending on how it goes with YouTube."

"He has an exit plan in case they cancel it, right?" I ribbed.

She fixed me with a stern glare. "Of course he does. Niall knows how much I hate when shows get canceled and there's no closure." She patted her belly. "I gotta get going, though. I've got about another ten minutes before I have to pee again, and I'm starving."

"Tell Niall hello for me," I told her, giving her a kiss on the cheek.

"Tell Noah—" She winced. "Sorry, Levi. It's habit. Tell Joey he and I are overdue for an ice cream date."

"I will." I smiled at her, held up a hand in departure, and headed toward my room for the night. I'd known Octavia since she first started as a scrub nurse. After our first surgery together, when we'd lost our car accident patient—the first time she lost a pediatric patient—I'd invited her and her then-fiancé to dinner. The four of us hit it off, and for years we alternated houses at least once a month. Noah and I hung out with Octavia and Niall almost as much as we spent time with Theo and Pamela. Since the divorce, though, the get-togethers were few and far between.

My friends were just as bummed as I was.

I eased into the on call room, leaving the light off in case anyone else was in there sleeping. One of the interns had grabbed my bag from the lounge and left it on a bed to stake it out for me. In exchange, I'd give them preference for scrubbing in for the next week.

I found the bag right where it should be. Not bothering to kick off my shoes, I swung into the bed, shoving the bag to the side. There was no blanket on my bed, though—a common occurrence in a place where the air conditioning was always jacked up. People were always stealing them, staff and patients alike. I'd come prepared, though.

Unzipping the overnight bag as quietly as possible, I felt around inside for my UConn Huskies hoodie. I wasn't the biggest college football fan, but the inside was lined in sherpa. It was the warmest hoodie I'd ever owned. Instead of soft cotton, though, my hand closed around something tiny, smooth, and silky.

I pulled it out, setting the item on my lap and reaching for my phone. The flashlight would be too bright, so I woke up the phone and used the screen to illuminate the object.

"What the . . . ?" I gaped at the thong in my lap. I'd recognize it anywhere.

Noah bought it during our honeymoon.

A groan resonated throughout the room as a sleeping figure turned away from my phone's light. I shut it off, still holding the thong in my other hand. How it'd gotten into my duffel bag was a mystery.

Unless someone put it there.

I tipped my head back. Joey, maybe. I couldn't fathom my six-year-old knowing the significance of women's underwear yet, though. I mean, he was smart for his age, but thankfully he still possessed the naïveté of childhood. More than likely, if he put anything in my bag, he might've tried faking a note.

Joey wasn't the only one who wanted us back together, though. Our housekeeper Alice had purposely mixed up our sheets that first night when she did laundry. When I asked her about it, she just shrugged and turned away. Not before I saw the mischievous glimmer in her eyes, though.

I was gonna have to have a talk with her.

I definitely couldn't sleep anymore, not with those panties burning a hole in my hand. Sighing, I gathered my things, practically burning a hole in my brain trying to figure out how to explain it all to Noah.

I grabbed coffee from the attending surgeons' lounge and headed out. The rising sun painted the sleeping town in a hazy glow, the rosy orange filtering through a thick blanket of fog. Noah would be up—I knew it. She always rose early to sneak in some work before Joey popped up like a daisy.

The kid was like me in that respect—he woke up full throttle, and didn't stop until he laid his head down at night. I loved it. I'd been an outcast my entire life, and finally I had a carbon copy to share my oddities with.

Pulling into the driveway, I noted the light in Noah's kitchen. It would've sucked if she'd decided to sleep in. I took a deep breath, grabbed my bag, and got out of the Tesla.

At the door, I raised a hand to knock, then lowered it. I didn't want to wake Joey. My phone was in the car, though, and my eyes throbbed as if they'd been replaced with sand bags. I moved around to the kitchen window and tapped lightly on the glass.

Noah jerked the curtains aside, her glare adorably menacing. She held a large chef's knife in one hand, brandishing it at the window.

I grinned and waved.

Though I couldn't hear her, I read her lips loud and clear: "You're an asshole." Still, when I waved her toward the front door, she scowled and left the window. A few seconds later, the front door creaked open. I met her at the threshold.

"Sorry," I said in a low voice as I ducked inside.

"I could've stabbed you," she hissed.

"Thankfully I always have my suture kit." I smirked as she shook her head at me.

"What the hell are you doing here anyway? I thought you were staying overnight? Did you lock yourself out?" she asked in rapid fire.

I'd never seen her so wired. I really scared her. The grin fell from my face. "I didn't mean to startle you."

"It's okay. Just text next time." She nodded toward the kitchen. "Coffee?"

"I actually have to get back to the hospital," I said. I'd regret the missed sleep later. Noah's kitchen enveloped me in warmth, though, begging me to stay. "I just came to return something to you."

"Return something?" she echoed. "What is it?"

My lips tugged up into a lopsided grin as I unzipped my bag. "Just these." I draped the thong over one of my fingers.

Noah's eyes darted between the thong and my face. Those kissable lips of hers puckered into an O of surprise, twitched into a half smile, then formed another O. "How . . . ?" Her usually creamy complexion flushed with pink. "Where did you get this?" she asked, voice husky, as she reached for the underwear.

I held them up higher. "It must've got mixed in the laundry." A lock of hair fell onto my forehead.

She brushed it away, then yanked her hand back. "Can I have it back? Please," she added, reaching for the thong again.

"Do you remember when you bought it?"

"How could I forget?" She bounced on the balls of her feet, fingers stretching up. My arms were longer, though, my fingers more dexterous. "Give it back." She glared.

She didn't seem mad, though.

"We went shopping," I said, beginning the story.

She rolled her eyes, but her smile remained in place. Settling back down on flat feet, she crossed her arms.

"I was trying something on in the men's fitting room."

"Jeans," she blurted, her face reddening even more.

"You do remember." My grin widened. "I asked you to come in, tell me how they looked."

"So I did."

"You did," I said softly. "And then?"

"Levi." Her arms dropped to her sides. She held out a hand. "Please?"

"Funny. That's what you said to me in that fitting room."

Tipping her head back, she sighed. "You're impossible."

I took a step closer. "I'd give anything to go back to those five days, when we barely had enough money for a honeymoon. We were happy though, Noah. Weren't we?"

"Yes," she said, voice barely audible.

Eyes zeroing in on those soft, pale lips, I ducked my head. "Can we ever be that happy again?"

Blinking, she leaned into me. "I don't know," she whispered, even as her lips met mine halfway.

I linked fingers with her, crushing the thong between our hands.

❧ 17 ❧

NOAH

My mind slid to a halt as Levi's lips engulfed mine. Hot and wet, they felt like a warm, moist towel after a hard workout. I hadn't even realized how much the muscles in my mouth needed it until his lips slid across mine, tugging my bottom lip between his teeth.

I gasped as every coiled muscle in my body unwound. He squeezed my hand where our fingers linked, his other hand roaming until it settled on my hip. Those hands had once been tour guides to my body. They still were.

Nothing ever changed.

He pressed hard against me, sending shocks of hazy tingles through every nerve. My free hand ascended, abandoning its limp dangle at my thigh to anchor to his shoulder. I didn't have to think. My body went on auto-pilot, falling into our old rhythm.

It was easy.

In the back of my head, though, alarm bells rang. Eyes closed, I pushed them away. The sound only amplified.

Joey's alarm.

I stepped back, our lips separating with a wet smack. Immediately my body missed the heat of his, even as shame spread through me.

"Well, thanks," I said, shoving the thong into the waistband of my pants.

Levi frowned. "What's—?"

"Daddy!" Joey stampeded out of his bedroom and into Levi's arms.

I stole the opportunity and snuck into the kitchen like a thief. Leaning against the counter, I bowed my head and closed my eyes. I must've lost my damned mind. I couldn't let our son catch us making out in my living room. I'd come too far. We all had. Joey was finally adjusting to his new routine. Hell, even I was getting used to having Levi upstairs. Somehow, we'd healed our broken family, creating something new.

Yet my lips felt warm to the touch, swollen with his kiss.

I pressed the pads of my fingers to them. People didn't accidentally make out after getting divorced. After signing those papers, my job was to start over. Move on. Yet I hadn't.

Neither of us had, not really. Then again, we were both too busy for dating. Maybe I needed to make time for it. I imagined sending Joey up to Levi's so I could go out to dinner with another man. It wouldn't be right.

"I'm heading back to the hospital," Levi called.

I jumped, whirling from the counter. He leaned against the doorway. Concern etched itself on his face, floated in his eyes. I couldn't tell what he was worried about, though. For all I knew, he was just anxious to get back to his patients.

He eyed me, searching my face. Maybe he wanted me to be the first to say something. I couldn't bring it up, though. Not with Joey watching cartoons in the next room. Besides, I didn't even know what I wanted to say.

If there was anything *to* say.

After several long beats, I gave him a tight smile. "Okay."

"Okay?" he asked, voice gruff. With what, I couldn't decide. He could just be tired. Or maybe he wanted to talk, and was annoyed that I was brushing him off.

I had to, though.

"Okay," I repeated with finality.

He stood there a moment longer. When I didn't say anything else, he turned and left. A few minutes later, I heard tires crunching over gravel as Levi pulled out of the driveway.

Not a moment too soon, either. Any minute, my dad was going to pull in. Turning from the door, I shifted my focus toward getting Joey ready. It was the last day before spring break. Soon enough I'd have an entire week to sleep in and slow down.

I put on more coffee while Joey ate breakfast, mentally prepping myself for the day. Thankfully, it was a half-day of school. The last few hours were for the teachers' workshop.

"Momma," he asked between spoonfuls of Cheerios, "how come Daddy was here?"

The front door burst open and my dad stepped in, saving me from answering. "Good morning!" He held up a tray of coffees and a box of donuts, all printed with the Elli's logo.

My dad had always been a morning person. For as long as I could remember, he'd stop on the way back from bringing my mother to work and get us some kind of treats. Even when it was still dark outside and hard to believe that daylight was near, Dad brought the sunshine.

He always had.

"Dad," I chided. "I made coffee. You didn't have to buy any."

Leaning in to kiss my cheek, his graying beard brushed my skin. "I did, actually." He winked at Joey. "Someone had to save us all from the sludge you call coffee." He passed a kids' hot cocoa to my son and then handed me a coffee.

"My coffee is *not* sludge."

"No," he agreed. "You're just trying to put hair on your chest."

"Yes. Yes I am." I lifted the lid and sniffed. "This is a pumpkin macchiato. I didn't even know Elli's was still making them." After all, autumn had long passed.

"Well, I asked for it special. Turns out they keep some on hand. There's a bit of a pumpkin obsession in this town."

"There *are* a lot of white people in this town," I mused.

"Elli's would have a riot on their hands if they didn't extend pumpkin coffee season," Dad quipped.

Joey's eyes bounced back and forth between us. "What are you guys talking about?"

"Son of mine," I said, dropping to one knee, "please save yourself, find some originality in your life. Save yourself from the pumpkin fever!" I stretched a hand out to him, my pumpkin macchiato clutched to my chest.

"Save yourself from the weird that runs in the Clarke DNA," Dad muttered underneath a smile.

"You guys *are* weird." Joey slid out of his chair and carried his empty bowl to the sink.

Standing, I backed up a few paces and leaned against the refrigerator. What precious little energy I woke up with had been devoured by my burst of silliness. "Go get dressed," I directed. Joey tossed me an obedient grin and bounded off to his room. My dad wasn't the only morning person in the family, apparently.

"One more day, kiddo," Dad said, squeezing my shoulder.

"Thank you." I lifted the coffee in a salute.

"What else are dads for?" He eased himself into a chair, grimacing as his knees struggled to bend.

"All the driving back and forth can't be easy on you," I said as casually as I could.

He waved me off. "If things were different, I'd still be driving all over the place."

"What do you mean?" I tucked myself into a chair across from him. Lifting the lid of the box, I peeked at the donuts.

"There are a couple pumpkin ones in there."

I closed the lid. "I shouldn't." Donuts, muffins, and bagels—my three favorites, and the three foods that went straight to my ass. "What did you mean about driving everywhere?"

He shrugged. "Just an idea I once had. It was a long time ago."

"So humor me." I rested my chin in a hand. "We've got a few minutes."

"I don't regret staying home with you and your sister for even a second," he said, the crow's feet at his eyes tightening.

"I know that, Dad. But?" I pressed, patting his hand.

"Your mother went to med school and I went to veterinary school," he said, "then we found out your mom was pregnant and I made a choice. I wanted to give her the best shot. There weren't many women in the field. There still aren't—especially in positions of power."

I'd heard this story before. But where it'd made me swoon as a teenager, that my dad could be so selfless, it made me angry as a mom. My mother got her career, all right—at the expense of her children. She'd never been around. Surgery always came first, even before her marriage. I'd never been able to admire her because she'd all but abandoned us.

"I used to have this idea," my dad went on. He sipped his coffee, his eyes drifting away to somewhere else, a distant past. "Lots of people can't afford to get their pets fixed. It's an expensive procedure yet it's highly recommended. It keeps shelters from getting full. It even saves some pets' lives." He glanced at me, blue eyes momentarily heavily. He was probably referring to the cat Brynn and I had as toddlers, Smoky. She got out and came back pregnant, and in the end she was too small to safely deliver her babies.

The whole litter died.

I swallowed. There wasn't an English word for a parent who lost a child. Goosebumps broke out along my skin. I didn't remember Smoky's pain, but my dad often said that she cried for days after. I knew how deep my own pain would run if something happened to Joey.

Clearing my throat, I wrapped my cold hands around the paper cup of coffee. "So what was your idea?"

"I thought it'd be cool to get a van," he said.

"A van?"

Dad nodded. "Maybe it's the '70s kid in me, but I always wanted to refurbish a van. Make it a sort of on-the-go vet clinic. I'd travel from county to county and offer inexpensive veterinary services."

"That's actually genius, Dad."

He rubbed the back of his neck. "Yeah, well, someone else thought the same. A husband and wife vet team have a pretty popular van here in town."

"I'm sorry," I told him, meaning it.

"I'm not." Those blue eyes crinkled at the edges as he smiled. It warmed me down to my toes. It always had. "I've got a beautiful family, and my wife is on track to be the next Chief of Surgery. No complaints here." He stood as Joey bounced into the kitchen.

"Ready, Pop?" Joey asked, zipping himself into his coat.

"I am." My dad put a warm hand on my arm. "There's always something you have to sacrifice when you're on the chase. For your mother, it was her family life. For you, it was your marriage."

"Don't compare us," I snapped.

"I'm just saying you two have a lot in common. She misses you, you know. You should bring Joey over for dinner sometime."

"When? Between surgeries?" I stood too. "Thanks for taking Joey to school." I kissed my son's head. "I'll see you both later."

I watched them leave, then sighed in the empty kitchen. I wasn't like my mother, but I'd married a man just as absent as she'd been.

Grabbing my things, I considered the donuts on the table. They were too tempting in my kitchen. I put the box on top of the load I already balanced. I'd stick them in the teachers' lounge. They wouldn't last the day in there.

Eventually, I should give up my anger. Let go of all of the resentment I carried. Maybe even open my heart back up to my mother. Her presence in my life amounted to traces, though. I didn't know how to forgive a ghost.

It wasn't as if she was making any sort of effort, either. If she really told my dad that she missed me, it must've been offhand, the way I sometimes mentioned that I should clean my oven. I never actually did it.

My mother was more present in her grandson's life than she'd ever been in mine or Brynn's. I'd learned to be okay with that, to accept that some people made better grandparents than parents.

I wondered if Levi would be a good grandfather to Joey's kids, or if he'd work his way up to Chief and never be heard from again.

❦

IT WASN'T UNTIL LUNCHTIME THAT I FOUND THE THONG STILL tucked into my pants.

I stood in front of the microwave in the teachers' lounge, watching the glass plate spin my leftover meatloaf around. Something dropped down the leg of my pants. Jerking back, I lifted my leg, half expecting to find a used dryer sheet. The silky panties pooled at my ankle. I closed my eyes, heat rushing to my face.

Turning in slow motion, I checked my co-workers' reactions. Dust floated down in the fluorescent light, swirling as it reached the floor. Blood pounded in my ears, and I groped for some way to defend myself.

Thankfully, they all sat immersed in their own lunches and the day's gossip. Sometimes, the teachers were worse than the children.

Especially when they talked about their own students.

"He's such a little shit," Jessica, a math teacher, said between mouthfuls of her kale salad. "I swear to *God* he wants to make me miserable. In between sleeping at his desk he tells me how much he hates math. Over and over."

I didn't bother reminding her that the student she was talking about had recently lost his mother. Teenagers were already apathetic about the quadratic equation. Throw in losing a parent, and it was a miracle the kid even came to school. More than likely, he was struggling with untreated depression.

We'd had this conversation before. At least, I had. My words always fell on deaf ears, and complaining to my principal got me nowhere. I loved my job, and I loved my students, but I hated how catty some of the teachers could be.

Crouching over as if I were tying my shoe, I snatched the thong and stuffed it into my lunchbox as stealthily as possible.

"And Asia," Jessica went on, mispronouncing the girl's name. It should've been Ah-*shay*, but Jessica insisted on saying it like the continent. "She wore another tank top with her bra straps showing today, and I had to stop my whole class to send her down to the office for a change of clothes. *Again.* Of course, they couldn't get the mother to bring anything in, so they gave her some of the *donation* clothes." She rolled her eyes. "She spent the rest of my class pissing and moaning about how I'm sexist and ruining her education."

"Your attitude is pissy," I muttered, balling my hands into fists. The microwave *ding*ed, but not soon enough to drown out my words. I pulled the hot container out.

"Do you have an opinion, Miss Perfect?" Jessica sneered. "Oh, wait. You're *not* perfect. You're divorced—and still living with your ex-husband!"

The container seared my fingers, and I involuntarily let go. It landed on the table with a thud, splashing ketchup onto her crisp, white shirt. Her jaw dropped open with shock.

"Oops," I said, suppressing a laugh. "I guess you're right, I'm really not perfect!" Grabbing my lunch, I left the lounge, preferring the quiet of my empty classroom.

A year ago, I would've ran from the room, hands shaking from her cutting remark. I wasn't ashamed of my divorce, though. I didn't care if I didn't impress those small town women with their small minds and even smaller hearts. What Levi and I had worked. It didn't matter what anyone thought.

As if to illustrate my epiphany, my phone vibrated in my desk. I pulled open the drawer and read the words on the screen.

> << **Levi:** *I'm headed home. Do you need me to pick up*
> *anything on my way?* >>

I couldn't remember him ever asking, not in our six years of marriage. It'd never occurred to him to do so. He assumed that, if we needed something, I'd get it in my weekly grocery shopping trips.

Right in front of my eyes, he was shifting. He reminded me of the man I'd fallen in love with in college, the one who made midnight runs to gas stations on his bicycle to get me overpriced Excedrin for my finals-induced migraines. I never even needed to ask.

Our situation might be strange, but maybe it was exactly what we needed. And maybe his question meant more than "Do you need anything?" Maybe the answer he wanted was about our kiss.

Thumbs poised over the touchscreen keyboard, I considered possible answers. Words that could hold double meaning if I was right, but would be harmless if I was wrong.

My mind stretched back to those college days, when Levi, Pamela, Theo, and I celebrated with sundaes from Friendly's after especially trying exams. The family restaurant was a dying breed in an age of demand for experience restaurants—places like Buffalo Wild Wings where they'd put literally anything on chicken wings.

> << **Noah:** *The children—and by "children," I really mean*
> *the teachers—are testing my patience today. I could use*
> *a Friendly's Reese's Pieces sundae.* >>

I added a crying laughing emoji and a winking one, then followed up with a second text.

> << **Noah:** *We actually need milk, though, if you*
> *don't mind.* >>

Pressing the send button, I put my phone away, then cleared my desk in preparation for the last stretch of the day. In about an hour, I'd be home and on spring break. Teacher politics would be the furthest thing from my mind. With no grad school assignments to work on, I'd have the free headspace to actually work on my novel.

Not that there was much of anything to work on.

I was writing myself in circles. The story was going nowhere. I wasn't really sure what I was writing at all, anymore. I wanted to tell a story that really mattered, like so many of the YA novels I'd read over the years. Something that would reach into teens' hearts and tell them "You're not alone." Instead, I'd ended up with a muddled mess, as if a child had finger-painted with all the colors of the rainbow, the oranges and purples and greens running into each other to form an unappealing brown blob.

Just like my post-divorce life, it was complicated.

What wasn't complicated, though, was the ease of a half day before break. My students were more than happy to watch the first half of *The Hunger Games* and even tolerated my literary questions every few minutes.

With no assignments to grade, I got to leave after the short professional development meeting. I drove home singing along to a pop song on the radio that I'd never admit out loud that I liked. When I pulled into my driveway, Joey waved at me from the upstairs window. When I waved back, he motioned for me to come up.

I hesitated. I hadn't seen Levi since the kiss. We hadn't spoken, apart from our short text exchange. I didn't want our son to pick up on the awkward tension between us.

Joey's waves grew more insistent, though, making him look a bit like a broken wind-up toy. Shaking my head in defeat, I headed upstairs.

He met me at the door, his hands closing around mine and tugging me into the kitchen. "Momma, come on, come on!"

"Jeez, kid. I don't think Daddy wants me tracking dirt all

through his house." I halted long enough to kick off my boots, then let him pull me along.

"Sit, Momma," he instructed, leading me to a chair.

"What's gotten into you?" I laughed. "You're awfully bossy today."

"Just close your eyes."

I glanced around for support from Levi, but he was nowhere to be seen. "Where's Daddy?"

Joey exaggerated a sigh. "Just close, Momma! And no peeking."

Shrugging, I did as he told me, even putting my hands over my eyes to show that I was not, in fact, peeking. The kitchen settled into silence, until Joey started singing at the top of his lungs. Beneath the lyrics to Etta James's "At Last," though, I thought I heard chuckling.

"Can I open my eyes already?" I asked, intrigued.

The singing stopped.

"Just a second," Joey said, drawing out the word. "In five . . . four . . . three . . . two . . . one!"

Small hands closed around my wrists, pulling my hands from my face. I kept my eyes closed, though, teasing him.

"For someone who wanted my eyes shut so badly," I said, reaching out to where I thought he stood, my fingers wiggling, seeking ticklish ribs. My hands met firm, warm abs, though—Levi's.

I opened my eyes.

"You," I said. Fingers splaying, my hand remained on him as if magnetized.

"Here I am." Levi grinned. "Still in shape, too, even though you're making me eat ice cream in the middle of the afternoon."

"I'm not making you do anything." I drew my hand away, swatting at him. "What do you mean, ice cream?"

He nodded toward Joey, who held out a Friendly's to go cup.

"Surprise!" our son said, pushing it into my hands. "Daddy said it's your favorite."

I peeked through the clear bubble lid. Sure enough, Reese's

Pieces and whipped cream pressed against the hard plastic. Blinking, I tipped my head back until my eyes met Levi's.

"I got milk, too," he said softly.

Staring into those brown eyes with a sundae in my hand, I knew I was in trouble.

✿ 18 ✿

LEVI

"Alice," I said in my best Ricky Ricardo impression, "you have some explaining to do."

My housekeeper looked up from the bottom shelves she dusted, shelves stuffed full of my medical books. Her glasses slipped down her nose as she looked up at me, an eyebrow raised.

"The jig is up." I knelt in front of her.

"What jig?" The hazy afternoon light filtering in through the windows made her look decades younger. It couldn't hide the glint in her eyes, though.

"You can drop the act. I know what you're doing." Gently, I took the rag and can of Pledge from her, then pulled us both to our feet.

"I don't know what I'm doing," she said, though the corners of her mouth twitched. She tucked her silver bob behind her ears.

I tilted my head at her the way I looked at Joey when I caught him fibbing. "The missing sheets? Busted hot water heater? My favorite henley that I never found? Noah's, erm, panties in my duffel bag?" I crossed my arms. "Come on, Alice. 'Fess up."

She tossed her hands into the air. "Oh, fine. I really had

nothing to do with that hot water heater, though. It was a fortunate coincidence." She grinned, dentures pearly white.

I shook my head at her, and her face fell.

"Oh, Levi. I really didn't mean anything by it." Wringing her hands, she dropped into the recliner I'd taken with me from the old house. "I just want you to be happy."

I sat on the arm of the couch. "I know. I guess I should be thanking you."

"Oh?" She leaned forward, eyes eager behind her glasses.

I chuckled. "You've got to stop, though."

"Oh, all right." Alice waved a hand at me. "This old lady's gotta get her kicks somehow."

"Alice, you are far from old. You're the best scrub nurse in the hospital."

"I'm retiring," she announced.

The arm of the couch dug into me, making my butt go numb. I shifted. "Retiring?"

She waved a finger at me. "Don't act so surprised. No matter how many times you tell me I'm not *old*, I'm still seventy-one. They've been trying to get me to retire for years. Why do you think I'm doing people's laundry? I can't just stop working."

"I get it," I said, standing. "Do you want some coffee or tea? I feel like this is a hot beverage conversation."

"Oh you sweet boy." She stood too, rising onto her tiptoes to pat my cheek. "I've got a wife and grandkids to get home to. Someday you will, too."

"I hope so."

৩৫৩

MORE OFTEN THAN NOT, I SPENT SATURDAY MORNINGS AT THE hospital. That weekend, though, I slept in for the first time in years. I woke up around eight, the quiet neighborhood fluttering around me like a heartbeat in utero. I quickly pulled on sweats and a long-sleeved henley, then descended the stairs with two cups of coffee in hand. Noah's favorite: a Keurig mocha latte that she drank every morning when we were still together. I knew she hadn't bought them since. Joey told me she always said they were too expensive.

Shifting the mugs around, I knocked on her door. The steam wafted into the air in a continuous S shape, carrying the scent of coffee and chocolate to my nose. When no one answered, I leaned toward the door, listening. I'd figured they'd both be awake already, but maybe I'd been wrong. As I debated whether to knock again or go back upstairs, the deadbolt clicked back and the door swung open.

"Daddy!" Joey announced. He reached for my arm to draw me inside, but I held the coffee mugs in the air.

"Careful, bud. It's hot. Can I come in?"

Noah padded into the kitchen. "Who is it, Joey kangaroo?" Her voice, thick with sleep, wound around my heart, squeezing with enough pressure to make my chest tingle.

Joey opened the door wider. "Daddy brought coffee," he told her in a singsong voice. "It's your favorite."

Ducking my head, I held a mug out to her. Leave it to my kid to blow up my spot.

Slanted eyes studied me as she took the cup. Noah inhaled, her eyes closing in dreamy bliss. "Oh my heavens, is this Gevalia?"

"It is." I glanced down at Joey, whose head swiveled back and forth as he studied both of us. He reminded me of an owl, his eyes so wide with hope.

I knew he'd struggled with the divorce at first. On too many nights at the hospital, my phone vibrated with texts from Noah about our son, crying for me. For us.

Texts that I never answered.

I hadn't known how to respond. I couldn't see that all they needed from me was any sort of acknowledgement. Instead, I let anxiety stir my thoughts around until I either stood frozen or buried myself in a surgery. I'd learned that wasn't how to handle things, though. I just hoped that it wasn't too late.

"I got you a box, too," I said. I'd forgotten to bring it down with me. "It's on my counter."

"I'll get it!"

Before either of us could answer, Joey raced around me toward the stairs.

Chuckling, Noah moved aside. "Come in."

We sat at the kitchen table. Far above our heads, Joey's feet stomped through my apartment. If it sounded loud from the first floor, I could only imagine how it sounded on the second floor.

Noah winced. "Our neighbor is going to hate us."

"I haven't even met him yet," I admitted, leaning back in my seat. "Is he the grumpy old man type?"

"He seems nice." She shrugged. "Those little elephant feet would wear down a saint's patience, though."

It was my turn to laugh. "I'll talk to him, if he complains."

She nodded. "Thanks for the coffee."

"No problem." I tapped my fingers against the side of my mug. "I also came down to let you know I can take Joey. If you want."

"He might wear a hole through your floor," she joked. "He's been restless all morning."

"All?"

Sapphire eyes flashed, whether in amusement or annoyance, I couldn't tell. "He's been up since 5:30." A sleepy yawn parted her lips. With her features not quite awake yet, she looked softer. More open.

I wanted to take her to bed and hold her in my arms until she fell asleep. Instead, I let out a low whistle. "Doesn't he know it's his day off?"

"Joey never takes a day off." She smiled. "He's like you."

If she meant the comment to sting, I couldn't tell. "Well, he might be the only workaholic in the family now." Her eyebrows knitted together. "I'm off this week, too," I explained.

"You are?" Joey crowed from behind me.

I turned in my seat. He stood in the doorway, the box of K-cups tucked under an arm. "I am, Mr. Wester. Is your schedule full, or are you free to hang out with your dad?"

"Can we go sledding?" He raced across the kitchen and set the box on the table. "I'll get my snowsuit, and mittens, and— Momma, where are my boots?" A string of questions continued as he darted out of the room.

Noah held her mug to me in a salute. "Good luck."

I rubbed my face. "The snow's too hard for sledding. I'll go tell him before he tears the place apart." As I stood, though, a thought occurred to me. "How would you feel about him going skiing?"

"You're going to teach him to ski? Hasn't it been years?" she teased.

"More like a decade." I scrubbed at my beard. "I could teach him snowboarding. Skiing would be safer, but I'm not sure he'd go for the kids' harness."

"Why don't you sit down with him and research it?" she suggested. "Show him some videos on YouTube. He likes that family, the one that's always going skiing."

I stared at her blankly.

"He'll show you. YouTube is like TV now." She waved a hand at me.

"I know that. I show my residents surgical videos all the time."

"There are surgeries on YouTube? Graphic?"

"They're educational," I explained. "Not violent."

"No," she said slowly. "I just mean . . ." She sighed.

"You don't want him to be a surgeon." I crossed my arms.

"I didn't say that." Still, she gazed down into her coffee as if it were playing videos.

"He's been reading your mom's books. Mine, too. Like it or not, Noah, it's in his blood."

Color flushed her high cheekbones. "I know that," she snapped.

"Why do you hate it so much? We should be proud of him.

He's a smart kid. I was like that—I needed to know everything about medicine. I saw a doctor on Sesame Street and soaked it all up like a sponge. Except, back then, all I had were the dusty old encyclopedias on my grandparents' shelves." I paced the linoleum floor. "He has a real opportunity if you let him take it, Noah. He can go to Career Academy in Waterbury."

She stood, shoving her chair back. "I thought you were too good for public schools. All this time, I've been having my dad drive him back and forth out to Stems and Ivy, and you want him to go to a public high school, anyway?"

"I want him to follow his dreams, Noah. The same way I chased mine. The same way you're pursuing yours!" I spoke slowly to keep my voice low, but hot blood surged through my veins. She always took every opportunity to jab at my education and upbringing.

"What if he doesn't want to be a doctor?" She put her hands on her hips. "What if he wants to be a—" she glanced around as if looking for inspiration, "—a chef? Is that good enough for you? Are *we*?"

As the words tumbled out, she pressed the pads of her fingers to her lips. Tears shone in her eyes. She turned away.

"Noah," I said tenderly. "Is that how you think I feel?" Crossing the room, I cupped her shoulders.

She bowed her head, her back still facing me. Her body trembled.

"Both of you," I began, "are my entire—"

Our son slid into the kitchen in full snow gear. Arms spread wide, he beamed up at us. "Ta-da! I found everything all by myself."

Noah's shoulders shook.

Grimacing, I turned to Joey, mind spinning with damage control. Accusing eyes bounced from me to her as he put the pieces together. I couldn't explain why his mom was crying, though. I wasn't even sure why. Somehow, I sensed that it was my fault. I suspected that her single question lay at the root of every-thing between us.

Are we good enough for you?

There was no way to explain those complicated feelings to a six-year-old. I needed time to wrap my head around it all before I could explain it to myself. I needed to talk with her, to sit down and hash it all out. Our son needed answers, too, though.

"Did you make Momma cry? *Dad?*" He climbed to his feet, eyebrows furrowed.

But as Noah turned, there were no tears streaking her cheeks. Her lips curled upward, and a laugh tumbled out. She turned to me.

"Before he tears up my place, huh?" She shook her head.

I smiled back, relieved that I hadn't hurt her—again. "He works fast."

"I'm not crying, Joey," she explained, kneeling in front of him. "I'm amused."

He blinked. "I don't get it."

"It's a mom joke," she said.

"A dad joke, too," I added.

Joey groaned. "Not a dad joke!"

"You're right. It's not quite a dad joke." Noah kissed the top of his head, her eyes meeting mine. Her lips didn't move, but the message was clear.

We needed to talk.

❧

I SPENT THE DAY WITH JOEY AT MOUNT SOUTHINGTON. THEY offered ski lessons for kids, but we'd arrived at an in-between time. I brought my own gear, then purchased everything I'd need to teach him at their shop.

There were some perks to being a doctor.

At first he hesitated, his small body stiff and awkward as I tried to teach him balance and shifting. He'd drawn a hard line in the snow when I suggested using a harness, so I had to get creative. I took him to a flat area empty of other skiers and snowboarders, and we practiced just moving in the cumbersome skis. After a couple of hours, he'd mastered staying upright and I felt confident enough to take him onto the bunny hill—the beginner's slope.

We took the lift, our feet dangling into empty air. Pine trees covered in snow passed beneath us. Joey gazed between his skis in wonder.

"It's like we're flying!" he said, pointing.

"Just wait 'til you're cruising down that slope. Then you'll really be flying," I promised.

"This is the best day ever, Daddy."

The ache in my chest that had been lodged there for the past year loosened a bit. I bumped fists with him, too moved to speak.

Our first run down the bunny hill together didn't go like in the movies. There wasn't any triumphant father/son moment where we glided down like sudden pros. Joey moved as slowly as a snail with me cruising beside him, coaching. His eyes squinted with concentration, his tongue poking out of the corner of his mouth into the cold.

Still, we made it down.

At the bottom, I scooped him off his feet and skied a short figure eight, whooping in pride. "You did it! You did it, Joey!"

He cheered with me, arms flailing in celebration.

"This calls for a new nickname," I said as I set him down.

Wobbling for a second, Joey righted himself. He skied beside me as we made our way to the lift down. "What kind of nickname?"

"Gnarly Joe? Joey the Ripper?"

He cracked up, nearly falling down in the process. "I wasn't *that* good, Daddy."

"I don't know," I said. "I wasn't as good as you on my first run." I hoisted him onto the lift and took a seat beside him.

"You weren't?"

"I was the *worst*." I shook my head. "Your Bapa and Grammy

couldn't even get me to go down the bunny slope. I was too scared."

He held up a hand. "Wait. Bapa *and* Grammy used to go skiing?"

"Used to?" I chuckled. "They'll probably come with us next time."

Round brown eyes lit up. "Does Momma ski too?"

"Your Momma's more of a warm weather kind of girl," I said. "She makes a mean hot cocoa, though."

"Are we going home now? For hot cocoa with Momma?"

"She's getting some work done, so you and I are gonna hang out today. My hot cocoa isn't too bad, you know."

"Okay." Joey shrugged.

I took this as a sign that he wasn't hating spending time with me, and we lapsed into companionable silence. It wasn't until we were out of our gear and in the car, heading home, that conversation between us got going again. I'd decided to let him be the one to lead the way, to show me when he wanted to connect. I wasn't going to push things—I already considered the day a success.

"When we get home, can we look at your books?" he asked as I gunned it up Southington Mountain.

The stretch of road had nothing to do with the ski resort we'd been at all day. It was just a steep hill that the locals had nicknamed. Going down it in the Tesla was a bit like flying down Mount Southington, so I appreciated the dub. I could've easily jumped onto I-84 and taken the highway to Route 8 to get us home, but I wanted the ride with my son to last a bit longer.

As we passed bare trees glittering in the setting sun, I chose my words carefully. I didn't want to shut down Joey's interest in medicine, but I also didn't want to disrespect Noah's wishes. "Some of those books are a bit over your head, bud," I said, picking my way through the delicate conversation.

Joey huffed in the passenger's seat. "I'm smart," he insisted. "I'm in advanced classes. I can understand your books!"

I glanced over at him. His brow wrinkled in determination, his eyes on me. Sometimes I was so proud of him yet so at a loss as to what to do with him. He *was* smart, potentially an actual boy genius. He'd been reading middle grade fiction by four years old. Some of the subject matter had been a bit over his life experience level, but he could still read it. At six, the kid read high school math books for fun, even if he didn't understand all of the calculations yet. He stumped his teachers at Stems and Ivy, even correcting them on facts they'd gotten wrong. Noah and I had agreed to treat him like a normal kid, but he wasn't normal.

Not even close.

"You're not just smart, Gnarly Joe. You're gonna work at NASA or something, someday. I know how much you appreciate my books, and I want to share them with you. But . . ." I trailed off, unsure of how to explain it. I didn't want to make Noah the villain. He worshipped her. Usually, I was the bad guy.

Maybe that's just how it had to be.

"I need those books for work," I explained. "They're actually in my office at the hospital right now, for my residents. I promise you, though, after dinner we'll go to the book store and get you some of your own."

"I don't want kids' books, though," Joey practically whined. He was still only six, after all.

"Maybe we can find real ones," I suggested. They had to have medical books for adults with casual interest—without the photos that Noah felt were too graphic.

"You're lying," Joey said, sniffling. "Your books are in your office at home."

"What do you mean?" I eased into traffic on Meriden Road. We'd hit I-84 spillover. I'd definitely get my longer ride, and it wasn't going to be fun, considering my pissed off six-year-old.

"I was just in your office this morning!" he shouted through a veil of tears. Twisting in his seat, he grabbed his backpack from the back seat. He unzipped it and tugged a familiar looking tome from its interior. "See? All of your books are at home." He dropped the book back into his bag, then shoved the whole thing onto the floor in front of his seat.

My mind raced for a response. He'd caught me in a lie, a white lie meant to keep things smooth between him and Noah. Instead, I'd only widened the gap between us.

"I'm sorry," I said, because it was the only thing I could say.

We drove the rest of the way home in heavy silence.

❧ 19 ❧

NOAH

The front door banged open. I jumped in my seat at the kitchen table, the pen I'd been writing with clattering to the floor.

"Hello?" I called out. "Joey? Levi?" As I pushed back my seat, the door to Joey's room slammed shut. A moment later Levi shuffled into the kitchen, looking sheepish. "I'll make some coffee," I said.

"You're an angel." He dropped into a chair, unzipping his North Face jacket. His chest heaved. Breathing a heavy sigh, he buried his face in his hands.

I stood at the counter, watching him as my secondhand Keurig sputtered to life. From that angle, he was no longer my ex-husband. He wasn't my husband, either. He was my son's father, as lost as I'd been in those first months as a single mom. I set down mugs of Gevalia mocha lattes, then sat across from him.

"Okay, co-parenting meeting. What happened?"

He rubbed his face, his stubble scratching against the palms of his hands. Against my will, my mind flashed to nights when his cheeks grazed the sensitive skin of my breasts as he worshipped my body.

I suppressed a sigh, wrapping my hands around my mug.

"We had a great day," Levi said at last. "You should've seen him on the bunny slope. He killed it." His eyes met mine, pride shining in them.

My heart squeezed, a faster rhythm pulsing through my veins. I swallowed, sat in patient silence, letting him work his way through it while I fought the urge to stand and hug his head to my breasts and caress his hair like I used to.

"He's smart as a whip, though, Noah. Stings, too." He shook his head. A lock of hair fell across his forehead and I wanted to brush it away.

Most of all, I wanted to comfort him. I knew how much he wanted to make things right with Joey again. I wanted it for them —and for us, too, I realized. It was all I'd wanted, even when I severed the connection between us, telling myself it was for the best. I just needed Levi.

In more than one way.

"What do you mean?" I asked him, voice throaty and obvious to anyone who paid attention. Thankfully Levi wasn't. His focus was on our son, like mine should've been.

"He won't let those books go. I told him he couldn't borrow them, that I'd get him some of his own. He said he didn't want baby books, and he hasn't spoken to me since." He shrugged, palms out and open on the table. "I know I shouldn't be complaining to you, of all people. I'm trying, here, though. I really am." His eyes met mine again.

Without thinking, I put my hands on his. The skin to skin connection lit up the part of me that had been dormant, pulses of ecstasy spreading through my nerves. His hands closed around mine, his eyes intent. He felt it too.

"It's just going to take some time," I whispered. "He loves you. Nothing—not even super cool off-limit medical books—can change that." I leaned toward him, the edge of the table digging into my rib cage. I didn't care, though. "I know you're trying, and he knows too."

"You do?" he asked, body tilting toward mine.

"Yes." I squeezed his hands, groping for the words. "Levi, I—"

Joey cleared his throat from the arched doorway. He held a thick hardcover book in his arms—one of Levi's books. On tiptoes, he inched toward the table.

Levi released my hands, turning toward our son. "Hey, Gnarly Joe."

I lifted an eyebrow at the nickname, burying my expression in my coffee mug as I took a sip. They were so close to bonding again. From the day Joey was born, Levi bestowed nickname after nickname upon him. Some of them—like Joey kangaroo—warmed me down to my toes. Others made no sense, but it was still cute. It was their thing.

Joey held the book out to him, his small arms wobbling under its weight. "Am I in trouble for taking this?"

Taking the book, Levi shot a questioning glance toward me.

If they were ever going to heal their relationship, Joey needed to see Levi as a full parent—including as an authority figure. I gave him a tiny nod, encouraging him to take point. My job was to back him up.

"Come here," Levi said, holding his arms open. Joey stepped forward, and Levi lifted him into his arms, settling him on his lap. "I know these books are really important to you, and I love that you appreciate them so much, buddy. I really do." He glanced at me.

I nodded, giving him the go-ahead.

"But," he said, looking Joey in the eye, "you shouldn't have taken it without asking. I do need them for work sometimes, and if I couldn't find one I needed, I might take out someone's eyeballs instead of their kidney." He made a mock face of horror, and Joey giggled.

A soft smile curved my lips upward. Seeing them together, even if Joey was technically in trouble, made me whole again. So much of me had been broken since I packed our things and left. It was strange to think that under one roof, we'd broken, yet under a new roof, we were healing. The house we'd made our home had become a sort of halfway house for us, easing us into a new chapter. I just didn't know what the story was yet.

Maybe it was up to us to write it as we went.

"Seriously, though," Levi said sternly, drawing both Joey's and my attention again. "You are not to take things from me, Momma, or anyone else without permission. That's stealing. Do you understand?"

Joey nodded. "I'm sorry, Daddy."

I pressed a hand to my chest, barely containing my smile. Tears pricked at my eyes, but I blinked them away.

"Am I punished?" he asked in his little voice.

Levi glanced at me.

Clearing my throat, I stepped into the conversation. "I think," I said slowly, visually checking with Levi to make sure he agreed, "you understand, so I think your talk with Daddy was sufficient."

"But," Levi added, "I don't want you slamming doors in your mother's apartment or anywhere else ever again. Do you hear me?"

"Yes," Joey said. He turned to me. "I'm sorry, Momma."

"Thank you." Standing, I smiled at him. "Let's go have a bath and get ready for bed."

Part of me expected Levi to disappear upstairs. He not only stayed, but he also joined in on the ritual, leaning over the tub to play with Joey, and tucking him into bed while I read from *Wicked*. When Joey's eyes grew heavy and fluttered closed, I turned off the light. Levi trailed me out of his room, easing the door to exactly one inch open—enough so that the light from the living room lamp trickled in but didn't hit Joey in the face.

"You remember," I whispered.

"Of course I do," he whispered back.

Standing in the dim room alone with him, I suddenly remembered our kiss from the other night. We still hadn't talked about it.

"Levi," I began again, the closeness of him tugging me into his orbit. The scent of his cologne and the fresh winter air from the mountain enveloped me, pulling me deeper into him. Before I realized what I was doing, I stood just inches from him. "We should talk about the other night."

"We should." He exhaled, his warm breath tickling my face. Then his hands were on me, one cradling the back of my head, the other on the small of my back. Eyes on mine, he closed the distance between us slowly, silently giving me plenty of time to pull away.

I didn't.

I swept my lips across his, then tugged on his lower lip. In college, I used to tell him I could kiss him all day, and I wasn't kidding. We once spent hours in his dorm room, just kissing. I left dizzy, lips bruised, heart open.

I wanted that feeling back.

Moving my hands to his shoulders, I pulled him closer. Those velvet soft lips of his took control, parting mine, deepening the kiss. His tongue sailed across my lower lip, and I turned to water in his arms. We moved as one, as if we'd melted into each other, backing into the couch. He fell back, sitting neatly and taking me with him. As my body curled around him, both hands cupping his face, his hands in my hair, my raw heart stitched itself back together with big, ugly loops.

The stitches were temporary. It was up to us to do the rest of the work.

"I miss you," I whispered against his lips.

The ardent look on his face told me everything I needed to know, but the honesty of his words gave me what I needed to hear. "I need you, Noah," he said, holding my face and looking deep into my eyes. "I've always needed you, but I wasn't here. I want to change that. I'll do whatever it takes to prove it to you. Nothing is keeping me from you ever again."

Speechless, I kissed him in response. I showed him with my mouth and my hands on his chest that I believed him, that I was willing to give him the second chance.

There was a good chance that I'd get burned again. Words meant so little. They also held great power, though. Every day they forged alliances or razed friendships. It all depended on how you used them.

I didn't have words to give him, not yet. All I could do was hope that with enough time and enough effort, the cuts that went deep into my heart would heal, that we really could be a family again. We could be *us* again.

So instead of words, I spoke with touches, using my mouth to tell him in other ways that I was willing to let him back in. Once, I'd lived for his kisses, high off just his lips and tongue. There was no way to go back, but for the time being I was content to ride the wave.

❦ 20 ❦

LEVI

After almost a full hour of making out, I untangled myself from Noah and kissed her goodnight. All I wanted to do was peel her clothing off and kiss every inch of her skin before sinking into her, but I knew she wasn't ready for that. I wasn't, either, truth be told. I hadn't been with anyone else since the separation and divorce. Neither my busy schedule or my bruised and battered heart allowed for it.

If it happened, I wanted it to be because we were both moving forward together. Sort of a renewal of commitment. I couldn't let myself hope for anything like renewing our wedding vows, but I at least wanted to know that we were invested in each other.

My heart couldn't take it if we weren't getting a second chance.

So I treaded lightly. Over the next few days, I spent time with my son, repairing our relationship and getting to know him. We ended up going to Too Odd, the book store on Main Street, and getting a medical textbook on physical examination. I spent a solid two days playing doctor with my son, except where most children had plastic doctor's kits, my son had his own real otoscope and stethoscope.

Joey was serious about medicine—more devoted than I'd been

in high school, when I'd taken a couple of pre-med courses at the community college (mostly because I wanted to check out the college girls). I definitely needed to revisit sending him to Career Academy with Noah. Stems and Ivy was great for him, but they didn't offer the kind of medicine courses he'd need in high school in order to get into med school.

The other option was Taft, right in town. Either way, it was more important than ever that I gave him a head start—as long as it was *his* dream.

I didn't want to pressure him into anything the way that Noah's mother had treated her. I knew it was a sore spot for Noah, but I also had to convince her that we needed to support Joey's dream. Even if that dream happened to fade when he hit middle school. For the time being, it was what he wanted.

I'd do anything for him.

For both of them.

So I gave Noah space and Joey time, spending those spring break days in a routine I'd never known. The more it became normal, the more I realized how badly I wanted it to never end. After full days with Joey, we'd troop downstairs for dinner with Noah, who usually stirred up some magic in her Crockpot. We stole glances and kisses when Joey wasn't looking, and I hoped there would come a time when we had to sit down with him and tell him we were back together.

We weren't, though, not really. In a way, we were just playing house, living in a dream bubble. While I didn't want it to burst, I wanted to take us out for a test drive. Otherwise, I'd never know if we were a "we" again.

On the fourth morning, I woke up and texted Noah.

> << **Levi:** *Don't cook. I'm taking us out tonight. Your choice.* >>

She replied right away, almost as if she lay in bed with her phone in her hands, thinking about me too.

<< **Noah:** *I can't, Levi. I don't have anyone to stay
with Joey.* >>

<< **Levi:** *I said "us." That means Joey too.* >>

Ellipses appeared, then faded. I watched my phone, eyebrows
furrowed. As the minutes stretched on, the hope ballooning in my
chest began to droop. Thirty minutes passed and she still hadn't
responded. Sighing, I got up, leaving my phone among the
rumpled sheets. The day had to go on. I had a kid in the living
room waiting for waffles. That morning we were going to try
adding leftover teriyaki chicken to the batter, taking our Will It
Waffle? experiment to the next level. He'd shown me Rhett and
Link taco videos and, even though they kind of turned my stomach, adding things like peanut butter and jelly to our waffles had
been benign enough.

Besides, Joey got a kick out of the whole thing, and that was
enough for me.

He looked up from the counter as I ambled into the kitchen.
Standing on a stepladder, he dug chicken out of the container of
stir fry. "Good morning, Daddy," he said, returning his attention to
the food.

"Morning, Gnarly Joe." I popped a K-cup into the Keurig and
let it do its thing. "I see you're all ready for our experiment."

"Almost. Can we vlog it?"

"Vlog it?" I echoed.

"Yeah, Daddy. You know, like video it."

"I know what vlogging is." I chuckled. "Who do you think
invented it? My generation, kiddo."

He eyed me dubiously.

"Look it up," I told him. "Why do you want to vlog this,
though?" The world really didn't need to see me choking down
teriyaki chicken waffles.

"I'm gonna start a YouTube channel," he said simply.

"Your username can be BoyGenius, and your first episode can be called 'Boy Genius Kills Father,'" I joked.

"Actually, my handle is ExperiJoey, and I'm starting with the Will It Waffle? series." He rolled his eyes at me, looking so cute in that moment, it took serious restraint to keep my face blank.

"Don't you have to be thirteen to have your own channel?" I removed my full mug from the Keurig and leaned against the counter. Tough conversations with my six-year-old and no response from Noah made for a black coffee kind of morning.

"You can fake your birthday." He shook his head at me. "I thought you said your people invented this?"

"My people?" I grinned. "Yeah, I suppose us old people seem like a whole different tribe to six-year-olds."

"Do you have a tripod?" he asked, eyes darting around the kitchen as if making calculations.

I needed more coffee if I had any hope of keeping up. "A what?"

He shook his head sadly, as if I'd told him I was out of Crunch Berries or school was now seven days a week.

"I'll just go get my phone," I said, setting my coffee on the counter. Parenting could be tricky. I held my composure until I was in the safety of my bedroom, my shoulders shaking with silent laughter. I retrieved the phone and out of habit, pressed the home button.

A new text from Noah waited.

<< **Noah:** *I really want to take things slow.* >>

Shoulders slumping, I dropped my hand to my thigh. The rejection stung, but I understood her reasons. Maybe I'd moved in too quickly. I should've given her more time. With one impulsive text, I might've ruined everything.

The phone vibrated in my hand. Holding it up, I read Noah's texts as they came in.

<< **Noah:** *I mean, it's not that I don't want to go out to dinner with you.* >>

<< **Noah:** *Because I do.* >>

More ellipses.

My heart thumped in my chest. If there was even a distinct possibility that I could smooth things over, I had to try. Flicking the screen over to the camera, I strode back into the kitchen.

"Joey," I said, sliding to video mode and pressing record, "how do you feel about me taking your mom out to dinner?"

He glanced up from his Crunch Berries, dropping his spoon into his bowl. Droplets of milk arced into the air, splatting on the table. Those round eyes of his widened. "You are?" His hands sprang into the air, fingers splayed. "Yes!" he shouted.

I texted Noah the clip.

<< **Levi:** *Say yes.* >>

Those damned ellipses appeared again. I sighed. "Well, buddy, we gave it our best shot." I sat next to him, putting the phone face down. "What's on our agenda for today?"

Joey cocked his head. "You're giving up?"

I lifted my shoulders. "She said no."

"Did she, though?" He squinted at me. "You always tell me I can't give up that easily."

"I know, Joey. This is different, though. There's a fine line between being persistent and being an asshole. Don't repeat that." I rested my forehead on the heels of my hands.

He patted my back. "Buck up, Daddy."

The front door opened and closed, and heavy, familiar foot-steps thumped toward the kitchen. I only knew one set of feet that heavy.

"Uncle Theo's here."

"Hurry!" Joey called to him.

I sat up, tipped my chair back, and retrieved my coffee from the counter. Suddenly even black coffee wasn't strong enough. I was nineteen years old again, getting shot down by the girl I'd been convinced I was going to marry.

Theo rounded into the kitchen, head swiveling as he checked things out. He hadn't been by since we first moved in. "Nice setup," he said. "You need curtains, though."

"Curtains?" I lifted an eyebrow at him.

He settled into a seat, his long legs and arms folding around my kitchen table like a giant in a dollhouse. "Yeah." He nodded like it was obvious. "They add that final touch."

"If you say so." I shrugged.

He elbowed Joey. "What's up with him?"

"He wants to take Momma out to dinner but he doesn't want to be *persistent*." Joey enunciated the word, using it in place of the swear.

"Well," Theo said, "did she give you a hard no?"

"What do you mean?" I nodded toward my phone. "I asked, and she . . ." Eyebrows knotting, I grabbed the phone, scrolling back through our conversation.

Theo and Joey leaned over my shoulder. I hit the lock button.

"Don't mind us," Theo said. "We're just coaching. Speaking of, y'all are looking at the brand new basketball coach at Watertown High!"

"Nice!" I high-fived him, while Joey scrunched his eyebrows at us. "What?" I asked him. "Are high-fives too 1990 for you?"

He sighed and turned back to his cereal.

"Anything yet?" Theo asked me, nodding at my phone.

"You're worse than a kid." Still, I unlocked my phone. Nothing. "I think it's a no."

He shook his head at me. "Don't make assumptions. Ask her if it's a no, straight up. And hurry up," he added. For the first time, I realized he wore his running clothes. "It's Tuesday, man. What's wrong with you?"

I'd completely forgotten. I'd become immersed in vacation mode, enjoying every second with my son. With Noah.

I couldn't keep all of my promises, though. Something had to give.

"Sorry, man," I said, texting Noah. "I've got Joey."

<< *Levi: Is that a no?* >>

Theo held up his hands, enormous palms out. He jabbed a finger in the air at me. "Uh-uh, buddy. You can't duck out on running day. We made a pact: no getting soft in the middle." He patted his belly.

He was right. Still, I couldn't send Joey downstairs. It wasn't even that I knew Noah needed to focus on work. I'd been enjoying our time together. I couldn't take my six-year-old on a run, though.

"What if we play basketball instead? Two on one?" I nodded to Joey, hoping Theo got my drift.

Theo snorted. "Y'all don't stand a chance." He stood. "Lucky for you, I'm not wearing my lucky basketball shoes, so you *might* actually score a shot on me."

Joey pushed his cereal bowl away, fixing Theo with dubious eyes. "If I sit on Daddy's shoulders, we're taller than you."

My phone vibrated and I snatched it up.

<< *Noah: It's not a no.* >>

<< *Noah: Okay.* >>

<< *Noah: I mean, yes.* >>

I pumped a low-key fist in the air.

"Then again," Joey remarked to Theo, "he's a little bit distracted today."

"You sure you don't wanna be on *my* team?" Theo asked him.

I made a dad sound before he could answer. "Uh-ah. That's not an option." I knelt in front of Joey, meeting his eyes. "We have a thing going here. Your geometry and my height. Don't be a traitor —we can beat him!"

Joey shrugged and Theo laughed, but I didn't care.

She'd said yes.

That one little word put wings on my feet. Joey and I beat Theo by just one point, boosting my confidence. Our date was going to be the slam dunk I needed to win Noah back.

❄ 21 ❄

NOAH

Just like that, I had a date.

I hadn't dated in years—since those college days when Levi took me to concerts and karaoke bars. Sometimes we just stayed in and watched movies in either of our dorm rooms.

Since the separation, I hadn't so much as looked at another man. There were a few reasons. I didn't have time, but mostly there was Joey to think about. Not to mention my bruised heart.

As the day drew to a close, I sat in my bedroom, staring into my open closet. Plenty of what I called "teaching clothes" hung in neat, rainbow organization. No date outfits, though. My only options were jeans, sweats, or teacher casual.

I grabbed a pair of blush high-waisted trousers that tied with a bow, pairing them with a short-sleeved white crop top. After dressing, though, I stripped right back down. It just didn't look right.

I was doing the thing I always did—letting my nerves about the date manifest into wardrobe panic. It was my tendency, had been my whole life. I should've called Pamela, but she and Theo were on their own date—or, as she called it, "impregnate and celebrate date." I didn't want to interrupt. With Theo steadily employed, they could get back to a stress-free Operation Baby.

Standing in front of the closet wasn't going to get me anywhere, either. I needed a good Pinterest session, but time was running out. Both Joey and Levi were upstairs getting ready, and they'd be down any minute.

The front door creaked open. "Reinforcements!" Pamela called.

My shoulders sagged with relief. "In my bedroom!"

She poked her head in moments later, whistling as she took in the clothing strewn all over the room. "Damn, girl."

"I know." It looked like a tornado came through. It'd probably be back, too. I flopped onto my bed, and Pamela sat next to me.

"Where are you guys going?" she asked gently.

"Just our favorite Chinese restaurant. I can probably get away with jeans, but . . ." I shrugged. "I'm pathetic, I know."

"Not even a little bit." Pamela tapped her lower lip, assessing my wardrobe. In her gray leggings and oversized blush sweater, she looked like the epitome of a snuggle bunny. She should be off somewhere cuddling and making babies with Theo. Standing, she danced around the room lifting articles of clothing and slinging them over her arm.

I watched the master work for a moment, then cleared my throat. "Pamela?"

"Hmn?" She held up a pair of dark gray leggings and black over-the-knee boots.

"Aren't you supposed to be out with Theo?" Smoothing a crease in the sleeve of a leather jacket I hadn't worn in years, I assessed the outfit she'd assembled on my bed.

The black leather jacket, a blanket scarf in a color I couldn't name—somewhere between olive green and gray—and the softest white T-shirt I'd ever owned, over the leggings. The outfit *was* cute, but it wasn't me. "Unless something's changed, isn't it a no-no to wear real leather?"

She scoffed. "What are you gonna do, give it back to the cow? You've had that thing for decades. Might as well wear it."

I shook my head. "Pamela, I can't pull this off. It isn't even a date outfit. It's too monochromatic."

"Exactly," she said, tossing the leggings into my lap. "It says 'I don't care, I'm just here for the food.' Hence the stretchy leggings." She held up a finger before I could interrupt. "*Plus*, you never try anything new anymore."

I obediently shimmied into the leggings, then pulled the shirt on. I had to admit: it was comfortable. I'd always liked the way that particular tee fell on my hips, how the soft cotton sort of just caressed my breasts.

"Your ass looks amazing. Levi should be thanking me for gift wrapping you."

I rolled my eyes at her. "Joey's coming with us."

"He has a bedtime, doesn't he?" She tossed me a wink.

I hadn't even considered whether I was ready to have sex with Levi. I'd barely even wrapped my head around the date. My body might be ready—I'd always been insatiable when it came to him— but my heart and mind were on different pages.

"Yeah, well," I said lightly, pulling on the boots, "let's focus that gettin' lucky juju on you. Where's Theo, anyway?"

She squeezed her eyes shut for a moment, then opened them. They trained on me, sparkling with amusement. "Promise you'll pretend to be surprised?"

I stood in front of the full-length mirror, checking out my reflection as I finished getting ready. I had to admit, Pamela knew what she was talking about. The black and white color scheme didn't wash me out like I'd suspected it would. With a pale pink lipgloss and a little blush and mascara, my dark hair long and loose, I looked exactly as she'd said.

Like I didn't care.

Like my entire future wasn't riding on just one date.

Because, whether I liked it or not, I'd never get over Levi. All I could do was try again, and hope for the best. Hope that things would be different.

"Levi needed extra hands. He's got Joey and Theo making a

trail of flowers from your door to the car."

I glanced at my outfit again. "Are you sure I shouldn't be dressing up more?" My stomach fluttered, a very real condition but one that neither Levi nor any other doctor could treat.

Since we'd moved into our apartments, I'd seen more effort from him than in the six years we were married. I could get used to it.

"You're perfect," Pamela assured me. "Now let's get you to that date." She held her arm out to me.

We looped arms and I nudged her with my shoulder. "And let's get you knocked up."

Grinning, she led me outside.

A carpet of pale pink flowers wound its way from the threshold to the running Tesla, its passenger door open and waiting. Levi stood beside it, a mixture of giddy excitement and hope on his face.

I bent to retrieve one of the flowers: a delicate apple blossom. Bringing it to my nose, I closed my eyes and inhaled its scent. A wave of memories rushed over me.

Playing outside as a child under the apple tree in our backyard. Lying in the bright green grass with my dad, making "snow" angels in the blossoms. Walking underneath a canopy of silk apple blossoms at our wedding—it'd been impossible to find the real things.

Yet he'd found them.

"How?" I asked, scooping up a handful of them and bringing them to my face.

"A magician never reveals his secrets." He and Theo exchanged conspiratorial winks.

Pamela stood to the side, hopping on the balls of her feet to stay warm. The frosty air stung my skin, but I still could've stood there forever. Against all of the odds, Levi had brought me a bit of spring.

The fluttering sensation in my stomach moved up into my chest. My eyes drifted up from the flowers in my hands to Levi. His grin widened.

I wanted to fling myself into his arms. With just one move, it was as if he'd undone all of the damage of the past few years. His careful surgeon's hands were stitching up my heart with each day. I smiled back at him.

The back passenger's side window rolled down. Joey's face appeared in the gap. "Are we going or what?"

"In a minute," Levi replied, not breaking eye contact with me.

"This isn't fun anymore," Joey grumbled.

Stifling a laugh, I released the blossoms in my hands. They drifted back to the snowy ground. Though I really wanted to stay and soak them in, there was a whole night ahead of me and the company of two sweet gentlemen to enjoy.

Even if one of them was getting a little hangry.

"Thank you," I mouthed to Pamela as I closed the distance between Levi and me.

She shot me a thumbs up, then scurried over to her and Theo's car. "Have fun, you crazy kids!"

Levi held a palm out to me as they pulled out of our driveway. I put my cold hand in his warm one, reveling in the warmth of his fingers as they closed around mine.

"Ready?" he asked in a low, gruff voice.

"Yes." Pressing a quick kiss to his shaved cheek, I ducked into the warmth of the Tesla. He closed the door behind me, leaving me to soak in the scent of his aftershave that clung to me.

I twisted in my seat. "Are you ready, Joey?" Even as the question left my lips, I knew I was really asking myself.

"Yes," he said, as if it were obvious.

Levi took us to New Wok, an unassuming but dynamite gourmet Chinese restaurant out in New Haven. It was almost an hour from home, but worth it.

It was surreal, coming back. Levi and I spent countless date nights in the tiny restaurant. One time, I'd been certain he was going to propose. The place was that paramount to our relationship. I hadn't been back since the separation, and neither had Joey.

It showed.

His finger moved down the list of menu items as he pointed out dishes to our server. We'd created a monster.

"All right, hold your horses," Levi said, lifting the menu from Joey's hands. "You can't possibly eat all of that by yourself."

"But I can," he insisted. "I need it!"

Levi looked to me for help.

"Well," I said slowly, glancing at the menu. All I really wanted was their sesame chicken. As long as I got at least a bite of it, I'd be happy. "What if we order a bunch of dishes and share?"

"Please, please, please," Joey chanted.

Our waiter laughed. "Would you like some more time?"

Levi ruffled Joey's hair. "I think we've got this." He rattled off our favorite dishes, including Joey's favorite—spicy mango chicken.

"And can I have an extra order of sesame chicken to go?" I gave Levi shifty eyes.

"I guess you're still addicted," he said.

"Or Momma's pregnant!" Joey sang out.

I nearly choked on my soda. Busying myself with mopping up my sweater, I avoided looking at Levi. Though I hadn't officially decided to work things out, I didn't want him to think that there'd been anyone else.

"Why would you say that?" Levi gently asked our son.

With a wink, the waiter took our menus and made himself scarce.

"Because," Joey said simply. "You guys are back together."

I dropped a napkin into my lap.

"It doesn't work that way," Levi began.

Though I felt his eyes on me, I said nothing, instead focusing on gathering the damp napkins. Maybe we'd gotten ahead of ourselves. I'd thought Joey would be elated to go out for a family dinner, but it'd never occurred to me that he might read more into it.

"And," Levi continued, "Momma and Daddy aren't *together* together. This is just us having dinner, as a family."

My skin tingled from his gaze. Taking a deep breath, I

glanced up.

Help me, his eyes pleaded.

"Daddy's right," I said to Joey, my voice catching on the words. "Do you understand?"

His lips twisted to the side as he worked through it. "So you're *not* having a baby," he said at last.

Levi coughed. I risked a glance at him. A mixture of longing and pain wavered in his eyes. I averted mine, instead focusing on my son.

I didn't want to give him false hope—either of them. Though my heart wanted to give Levi a second chance and I was willing to see how things went, my head cautioned taking it slow. The truth was, I didn't know *what* we were doing. It'd been reckless to bring Joey into it.

"When and *if* the time comes, I'll come to you and let you know. Okay, Joey kangaroo?" I smoothed his hair, missing the days when he'd been small enough to hold in my arms.

"Okay."

Fortunately, our server returned with our appetizers. Joey dove in, barely waiting for the waiter to put the dishes down.

From across the table, though, Levi's eyes met mine. He nodded to where my phone sat on the table. I'd put it on silent, but evidently he'd texted me. I groaned inwardly, fearing the questions, the need for talking.

I didn't want to talk or think. I just wanted to live in the moment.

Picking up my phone, I opened the text, bracing myself. A GIF from the Disney movie *Hercules* danced on the screen, a scene featuring Hades's hapless sidekicks.

<< ***Levi:*** *"If"? "If" is good.* >>

Despite my worries, I smiled.

AFTER GORGING OURSELVES ON SESAME CHICKEN AND FAMILY laughs, we gathered a sleepy Joey and headed home. Levi carried him into my apartment, our son slack and peaceful in his arms. My heart cinched around the image. The scene in front of me served as not only a memory, but also a glimpse into the future.

If I wanted it.

Levi ambled back into the living room, a hand rubbing at the back of his neck. "He's out cold," he said.

"Crack coma." I hung up my coat, turning my back to him for just a moment. It was all it took. When I turned around, Levi stood beside me.

"New Wok is nothing to play around with." His hands hovered at the zipper of his own coat, waiting for my instruction. His eyes begged me to tell him to stay. The heat of his body wrapped around me.

"It's risky," I said, no longer really talking about food.

"No turning back," he added.

I pressed the palms of my hands together, bracing myself. "Would you like some wine?"

"I don't think there's time." He stepped toward me and I turned into him.

The wall pressed into my back, the coats a cushion. "I don't think so, either," I whispered. As he closed the distance between us, I wrapped my arms around his neck. They settled into place, my elbows resting on his shoulders. His eyes darkening, he leaned in close enough that I felt his exhalations whisper across my lips, the question in his eyes.

I swallowed, hands trembling. I looked into those eyes and read only sincerity there. Just a quiet longing. I was the lock, and he the key, and if I let him in, there would be no going back. He'd changed, though. I could feel it, see it, and hear it. His transformation into a present father and partner was a tangible thing, in the smile on my son's lips and the cooling to-go food on the kitchen counter. I didn't want to go back.

I only wanted to run into my future with him.

In answer, I tilted into him and pressed my lips to his. Every nerve in my skin lit up, the light shooting through me. The rush knocked me back into the wall, Levi pressing against me. His lips fastened to mine, his hands in my hair. No words passed between us. We spoke only in the language of our bodies: the caress of a hip, the sweep of a tongue, the taste of salt and cool spring air.

His fingers roamed the waistband of my leggings, the pads skimming creamy skin. For a fleeting moment I was glad that I'd taken the extra time to moisturize after showering. The soft tee that Pamela had picked for me brushed across my belly, and a warm shiver tingled through me. Levi broke the kiss, eyes meeting mine again. I didn't need words or GIFs to know what he asked with those eyes.

Wordlessly, I nodded.

Twining my fingers through his, I pulled him into my bedroom. He closed the door behind us, its soft snick the only sound in the apartment. We stood in total darkness, the present eclipsing the past. No longer were we at war, sun and moon, Venus and Mars, Aphrodite and Ares. We were just a man and a woman.

Simple.

In the dim street light filtering through the curtains, I tugged off the T-shirt and my bra, dropping them to the floor. Levi watched in silence, his hands slack at his sides. His eyes roved down my cheek, stroking the curve of my breasts, gliding down the slope of my stomach. Eyes on his, I kicked off my shoes and slipped out of the leggings.

I stood naked before him, an offering.

It wasn't just my body I was giving him, though.

I backed toward the bed until my calves pressed against the frame. Then I laid myself down, dark hair fanning out around my face. My heart raced in my chest, breasts rising and falling with each rapid breath. I held out my arms to him.

Nodding, he shed his own clothing. His cock sprang free, pointing toward me, a compass in the dark. As he stepped forward, his foot found a stray boot. He wobbled, hands flying out as he steadied himself. Flashing me a grin, he found his balance. Then, his body as bare as mine, he came to me.

As he knelt on the bed, I rose up on my elbows, sitting myself up. He hesitated, freezing in place. My lips curled in a smile, reassuring him even as my heart thumped away. Gently I put my hands on his shoulders, pressing him back until he lay flat. He smirked at me as I crawled up his legs, my heat resting against him as I took my seat. His head throbbed against me and he closed his eyes.

I slid my body down his length, leaving a warm and wet trail. Levi moaned softly, eyes opening and finding mine. Lips parting, he opened his hands and I twined fingers with him as I slid back toward his head. Our hands curled around each other, eyes fastened. I ground my hips, moving back down. His hands squeezed mine.

"Condom," he whispered, voice rough with need.

"Birth control," I whispered back, sliding forward. As his head hit my notch, I lifted my hips and pivoted, taking him in inch by sweet inch. Even though it'd been well over a year, our bodies still remembered each other, fitting perfectly into place. When I'd sunk to the hilt of him, his head just at the threshold of my cervix, I swept my hips into a slow circle.

Levi's eyes fluttered shut, his hands tightening around mine. "No," he exhaled, and I couldn't tell whether he meant my name or he wanted me to stop. Then he thrust into me, hitting me at just the right spot. I rocketed out of my body and into a black velvet space, every nerve ending on the sweetest fire I'd ever tasted. He did it again, toeing the line between pleasure and pain as wave after wave pulled me under.

I bit my lip and clung to his hands, still trying my best to be quiet. Still, a whimper escaped as my body quivered with each orgasm.

"Do you want me to stop?" he asked, driving into me again.

"No. Yes. Don't," I murmured, regaining some control of my limbs. He released my hands and pulled me into him, his arms wrapped around me as my breasts settled against his chest. I clung to him, face buried in his neck and inhaling his clean, warm scent. On his next thrust, he jerked underneath me, throbbing inside of me. Hot fire shot into me, and I spasmed around him.

I lay on top of Levi, our hearts pounding against each other, our bodies still connected. Those surgeon's hands skimmed up and down my back, his fingertips still sending searing explosions across my skin.

I sighed contentedly. "It's too bad I don't write romance," I said, voice soft in the dark.

"Why's that?"

"Because that would've cracked my writers' block."

Levi wrapped his arms around me. "You'll get through it." He pressed a kiss to the top of my head.

"I hope so. If I can't write this book, then everything I've done is for nothing."

Beneath me, Levi stilled. My words echoed through my head, and I squeezed my eyes shut.

"I just meant going back to school to learn marketing," I assured him.

"I know." He kissed my head again. "So you don't want to teach anymore?"

I shook my head. "Don't get me wrong. I love it. I've always wanted to be a writer, though. I feel like I've just circled around it my whole life. Teaching lit to teens? I mean, come on." I chuckled, but my hands squeezed the pillow Levi's head rested on.

As our bodies calmed, his lips found mine again. "I love you, Noah," he said between kisses. "I want you to chase your dreams. I'm not leaving anymore."

"Well, actually," I told him, disconnecting our bodies, "you do have to sleep upstairs." I pressed another kiss to his cheek, then got up. Slipping into my bathrobe, I eased the door open. "Goodnight, Levi," I said over my shoulder.

As I padded toward the bathroom, though, I wished I could let him stay.

❧ 22 ❧

LEVI

I woke in our bed, stretching an arm toward what used to be Noah's side. Not anymore—but I hoped that would change soon. Even though she'd slept two floors below me, I lay there for several long moments, soaking it in as if she was right there with me. I longed to hold her in my arms for a whole night, for forever, but that would come in time.

I just needed to be patient.

I couldn't ask for more than what she'd given me, though. Lying there in our bed, I could still smell her skin on mine, and that was enough. Still, as much as I wanted to revel in it, a whole day stretched ahead—and we were both still on vacation. I showered and dressed, then found my phone in the pocket of yesterday's jeans. There were no texts from her, so I sent her one of my own.

<< **Levi:** *Breakfast?* >>

While I waited, I brewed a cup of coffee, my mind drifting with the possibilities. A hawk soared in the distant sky. Maybe we could make things work. Until the night before, I'd never dreamed that we'd be together again. Hoped, yeah. But that was a place I couldn't let myself visit for long.

As the Keurig spurted its final drops into the mug, I watched the hawk glide over roofs, disappearing into the distance. If I'd known we were going to get back together, I wouldn't have sold our house. Still, I could buy us a new one.

My phone vibrated in my pocket. With a silly grin on my face, I carried my coffee to the table, then tugged the phone free. A number I didn't recognize lit up the screen. Shrugging, I answered it in what Noah used to call my "doctor voice."

"Dr. Levi Wester."

"Hello, Dr. Wester. I'm Dr. Barbara Sheth, an attending surgeon with Stanford Hospital," a crisp, businesslike voice replied.

The rest of what she said was drowned out by blood roaring in my ears. As many times as I'd had to make The Call for one of my patients, I'd developed a fear of receiving it myself. I staggered into a chair, chest heaving. "No," I gasped. "Please."

"Dr. Wester?" she asked.

I gulped in air. The kitchen boiled like a furnace. If my legs weren't so weak, I'd go outside. I settled for the floor instead, dropping from the chair and resting my forehead against the cool linoleum.

"Dr. Wester? Are you there?"

"Please," I begged, as if that could make a difference.

"Sir, I'm not sure I—" She gasped. "Oh. Oh, I'm so sorry. Dr. Wester, no, everything is all right. My hospital is in California. I'm sure your loved ones are safe."

Blinking, I absorbed her words. "You're not calling with bad news?" I managed.

"I'm calling with good news, I hope," she said. "I do apologize, Dr. Wester. Please . . . If you need a moment to collect yourself, I can call back."

Legs shaking, I stood. Fatigue poured over me, and I collapsed into the chair again. "I'm all right." My voice sounded stronger, and already the color seeped back into the kitchen. I took large gulps of my coffee. I should've known better than to panic like that. Ever since Noah and Joey came back into my life, though, I was afraid of losing them. More than ever.

"I'm really sorry," Dr. Sheth said again.

I laughed. "Occupational hazard, right?" I shook my head, expelling the fears. Noah and Joey were safe. There had been no accident. There would be no phone call.

"Can I give you some good news?" she asked.

"Please," I chuckled. "I'm not usually this panicky."

"Oh, Dr. Wester, I truly understand. I think we all dread that call—especially when you've worked in trauma. I remember reading in your resume that you did your residency in a trauma unit."

"My resume?" My eyebrows furrowed. "What's this about?"

"I'm a surgeon at Stanford Hospital—the Chief of Urology. Long story short, a family emergency has called me out of the country, and I've promised my Chief of Surgery that I would secure a replacement before I fly out. I'm hoping that replacement is you."

I shook my head again. Two minutes earlier, I'd thought she was telling me that something happened to Noah and Joey. Suddenly she was telling me that one of the biggest hospitals in the country wanted me. Not only did they want me, but they wanted me to run their urology department.

The conversation was giving me whiplash.

"The board has agreed to fund your move across the country, of course, as well as housing for yourself and any family. I'm afraid we'd need you right away, though. I leave at the end of this week, and I'd like to meet with you in person to pass the torch, so to speak."

I drained my coffee mug and carried it back to the machine for more. "So you're telling me that Stanford is going to fly me all the way out to California?"

"Yes—and we still haven't even discussed salary." She ruffled some papers on her desk. "Now, we're a teaching hospital like Yale, so you'd be responsible for residents' education. I'm able to offer you a base salary of $436,000."

I choked on my first sip. Coffee spewed down the front of my shirt in hot rivulets. "Excuse me?" I put down the mug and reached for a towel.

"Of course, that's only to start with—"

It was twice my annual salary at Yale. With that kind of money, Noah could quit her job, drop out of school, and self-publish for fun. It wouldn't even matter if she sold a single book, because we'd be set for life. I could put Joey into whatever school his heart desired. I'd be able to afford the advanced education he so badly needed—education that even Stems and Ivy couldn't give him. I could even build us our dream home from scratch. We'd never want for anything, ever again.

That salary would solve all of our problems.

"Yes," I told Dr. Sheth.

"Yes?" she repeated.

I ran a hand through my hair, reminding myself that I should probably play it cool. They needed a urologist who could teach, and for some reason they wanted me. I needed to keep it together —at least until I got off the phone. "I'm interested."

"Excellent!" I could practically hear her smiling. "I'll get some paperwork rolling and I'll see to it that your flight is scheduled."

"My flight?"

"I'm going to need to have you sign a few things before we move forward," she explained. "I'll text you with the details shortly, and I'll have an Uber come get you at your address."

"Sure," I said, thinking of my breakfast text. Noah would understand, though. The opportunity would change all of our lives. One missed breakfast was a small sacrifice for the life we were about to begin.

After hanging up with Dr. Sheth, I checked my phone. One text and a missed call from Noah.

<< **Noah:** *I'm making bacon.* >>

"Shit," I muttered. My phone buzzed again.

<< **Dr. Barbara Sheth:** *Uber in 20, flight in 45.* >>

"Shit," I said again. Abandoning my coffee, I headed back to my bedroom, texting Noah as I made my way through the apartment.

<< **Levi:** *I can't make it. I'll explain later, but I have huge news. I love you.* >>

In the doorway to my bedroom, I stared at those three little words. They were only made up of eight letters, but their weight could make or break us. I hit the backspace button, editing with my thumb while I packed a bag.

<< **Levi:** *I can't make it. Something came up. I'll explain later, but it's big. I'll see you tonight—promise.* >>

I hit send, then prepared to face my future.

❄❄❄

I'D NEVER RECEIVED A JOB OFFER LIKE STANFORD'S BEFORE. I went to UConn and did my residency and fellowship there, and then got my dream job at Yale. I knew I was good. Yale only took the best of the best. No hospital had ever offered to relocate my entire family, though—or pay me half a million dollars a year. Throughout the entire flight, I kept waiting for the part where I woke up.

It never happened.

The plane landed and another Uber driver took me to Dr. Sheth's office. She stood behind an empty desk, the floor littered with boxes. Framed photos of her with various patients lined her walls. She held out a small hand to me and we shook.

"Please," she said, gesturing to the only chair that wasn't piled with items. As she sat, she smoothed the pleats of her high-waisted pants. "HR isn't finished with working on your contract, but I still wanted to meet with you and run you through some things."

She slid me several folders containing the hospital's various policies. For half an hour or so, she summarized the policies and made sure that I understood them. Then she stood.

"Shall I give you a tour?"

Stanford was bigger than I'd imagined. Dr. Sheth showed me around most of the areas I'd be working in, concluding with the residents' lounge. A group of residents rushed around the room in various states: a woman tied her shoes as she brushed her teeth; a man changed out of blood-soaked scrubs; another woman untangled her hospital-issued stethoscope.

"These will be your students," Dr. Sheth said. "You'll have urology fellows, of course, but at the moment they're in a conference."

I nodded, lifting a hand in greeting as most of the residents rushed past me. "Are the pediatric urology fellows also in a conference?"

Dr. Sheth's forehead wrinkled. "Sorry?"

"My pediatric fellows." I glanced around the empty lounge.

Dr. Sheth tucked her brown hair behind her ears. "I believe there's been a misunderstanding. Stanford Children's urology position is already filled. Your position would be for adult care."

I nodded, following her back to her office in a haze. Monster salary or no, I couldn't imagine not working with children. Pediatrics was all I'd ever known. Still, I couldn't exactly turn down the position just because I'd mostly be working with adult patients. I'd never receive another opportunity like it.

"I'm curious," I told Dr. Sheth while I waited for yet another Uber to take me back to the airport. "You know I'm a pediatric surgeon, right? Why not choose someone more qualified to be your attending?"

Dr. Sheth smiled. "You came highly recommended by your Chief of Surgery."

"Huh." I couldn't imagine humorless Dr. Combies praising anyone for anything. It was a huge honor.

"Believe it, Dr. Wester," she said. "Chief Combies and I were fellows here at Stanford together, and when I asked him if he had any recommendations, he said there was no one better than you."

Her words reverberated in my head as I flew back across the country. Fatigue gripped me tightly. All I wanted was a hot shower and a free fall straight into my bed. I needed to talk to Noah, though. The news couldn't wait and I had to see her reaction when I told her Combies actually liked me.

Despite the late hour, lights were on in her apartment. I sent her a quick text, then tapped gently on the front door. A second later, she pulled it open. I glanced past her into the living room, spotting a half empty bottle of wine and a full glass next to it.

"Can I come in?"

She moved aside, gliding back to her spot on the couch. She cupped the glass, the stem dangling between two dainty fingers. A delicate eyebrow cocked up at me, waiting.

"I'm sorry for taking off on you this morning." I sat next to her, angling my body toward her. "I got a phone call from the Chief of Urology at Stanford this morning. She wanted to fly me in immediately to talk about a job offer." I paused, gauging her reaction. She sat, silent. Maybe she didn't get it. When Noah didn't say anything after several more moments, I pressed on. "She wants me to take her position."

Her eyebrow twitched. She took a sip of wine.

"The salary is over a quarter of a million dollars." I watched her face for a reaction. She merely stared back at me. "They're willing to relocate us, too," I said.

Both of her eyebrows shot up. "Us?"

"Of course." Taking the wine glass, I set it on the table. I twined my fingers through hers. "The paperwork isn't ready, but it's as good as signed. We'll be in California by the end of the week."

Her hands stiffened. "The end of the week?" She shook her head. "Levi . . ."

"I know it's sudden. I'll take care of everything. You'll barely even notice we're moving." I grinned. "Just worry about that novel of yours."

Noah wrenched her hands from mine. "I'll barely even notice? Do you hear yourself, Levi?" She stood, pacing. "I can't just pick up and leave. I have a *job*."

My eyebrows furrowed. "I thought you wanted to quit, to be an author."

Pivoting, she put her hands on her hips. "Yeah—after I finish grad school." Though she kept her voice low, incredulous anger simmered beneath it.

I swallowed. "I thought you'd be happy. With that kind of money, we can do anything. You wouldn't even have to finish school. Joey could go to whatever child genius academy he wants. I'd come home and we could eat steak every night. Hire a personal chef. Get a housekeeper who doesn't play pranks." I laughed.

"You don't get it," she said, voice dropping an octave, words dripping slowly. "Nothing's changed. You're never going to change." She looked away, shaking her head. Her hair fell around her face, curtaining it from me. It couldn't hide how her shoulders curled like a shell—a barrier to fend off every advance I'd made.

I ran a hand through my hair, rubbing at the back of my neck. "You're right. I don't get it. This is a good thing, Noah." I touched her shoulder.

She wrapped her arms around herself, further closing herself off from me. "A good thing? You're never here. You up and disappeared today with barely a word."

"I texted you," I said. "They didn't give me much time for anything else."

"Joey was really bummed that you missed breakfast." She continued as if I hadn't spoken. "And lunch. Dinner, too. Without so much as texting us what was going on! And now you want me to drop my entire life, all so you can chase a job across the country?"

"It's a once in a lifetime opportunity, Noah," I snapped.

"No," she said, hugging herself. "This *family* was your opportunity."

I flinched. "What are you saying, Noah?"

"I'm saying what I've been telling you for the past six years," she hissed. "We need you. *I* need you—here with us. Not prancing around with a six-figure salary while we never see you."

I scrubbed at my beard. My head spun. There was just no pleasing her. I'd come home with the job offer of our dreams, the one that would solve all of our problems, yet she was accusing me of bailing out on her and Joey. "I thought you wanted to pay off our credit cards, student loans."

"My bills aren't your problem," she snapped.

My chest tightened. "Then what are we doing here? What's the end game, Noah?"

Her eyes burned into me. "There isn't one."

Jaw dropping open, I stood, wordless as my body absorbed the impact of her words. I'd never expected things to become perfect overnight, but I'd thought that we were getting somewhere.

I'd been wrong.

Raising both hands, I massaged my temples. There had to be a way to salvage things, to turn the conversation around. Yet there she stood, her heart as impenetrable as steel. Ever since we'd moved into the three-family home, it'd seemed like she wanted to repair things between us—especially after the night we'd spent together. I'd told her I loved her the night we got back together, but as I stood in her living room, I realized she'd never said it back.

Instead, she'd told me I had to go.

My chest burned. I sucked in a breath to quell the ache there, but the oxygen only fed the flames of grief. I had to know if she loved me, or if I'd just been kidding myself the whole time.

"Noah." I lifted my eyes to meet hers. "Do you love me?"

❧ 23 ❧

NOAH

California. He wanted me to drop everything I'd worked for and move across the country with him. For a job that would undoubtedly keep him away from Joey and me. After everything, he still couldn't see that we needed him. *I* needed him. I'd thought that he'd changed, but I'd been wrong. His career was still more important than his family.

Tears burned my eyes. I swallowed. I wouldn't let him see me cry. I'd hold them in until I could fall apart in privacy. He'd never get to see how he destroyed me, over and over again. I lifted my chin, nostrils flaring.

"You already took the job?" I asked, ignoring his question. I couldn't go there, couldn't say the words that matched the feelings that shredded my heart to ribbons.

"Yes," he said softly.

Somehow, that made it all even worse. I clenched my hands into fists at my sides. He hadn't even bothered to ask me what I thought.

"Come with me, Noah." His voice wavered. He held a hand out to me, eyes dark.

I wanted to ask him to stay. I needed him to tell me he'd been wrong, that Joey and I were worth following. Not the other way around. I was done asking, though. I'd known that for over a year, yet I'd still let my heart get in the way of what my head knew.

And Joey would pay the price.

I would, too, suffering in silence while I watched my son mend his broken heart again. It had to be the last time. I couldn't let Levi keep breaking promises. Even if I wanted to move to California, I knew what a new job meant. I knew the long hours that came with being Chief of Urology. He'd be gone more than he'd be home.

Swallowing, I placed my hand in his. I couldn't look him in the eye. There would be no happy ending here. Just a final goodbye, the closure that both my head and heart needed. That my body needed.

His fingers closed over mine and he dipped his head. Shadows flooded his face as he pulled my body into his. He wrapped one arm around me, his other hand still entwined with mine. Chest to chest, I felt the slow, defeated rhythm of his heartbeat. It echoed mine.

In silent sync, we backed toward my bedroom. With numb fingers I tugged at his tie. The door snicked shut, cocooning us in the dark. Levi slipped a hand underneath my sweater, those precise surgeon's fingers gliding across my skin as if absorbing its memory. I didn't want slow and sensual, though. I wanted to get him in and out of my system as quickly as possible.

Before the hurt I'd shoved down resurfaced.

With each button I freed, the ache in my heart only deepened. I wanted to rip his shirt open, flicking buttons onto the floor like shards of glass. Fisting the fabric, I inhaled through my nose. I just needed to keep it together until he left.

I exhaled, releasing him. Clothing dripped onto the floor. I pushed him down on top of it. He no longer deserved my bed. That safe place belonged to me only, reserved for later, to catch me when I finally fell apart.

Knees at his ribs, I lowered myself, taking him all the way in.

Moonlight washed us in pale streaks. He watched me with hooded eyes, hands gripping my hips as I moved against him.

"Noah?" His lips barely moved as he spoke.

I closed my eyes. If only there was a way to shut him out. Later I knew I'd wash him off my skin but he'd never truly be gone. Even once he was in California, I'd still see him every time I looked at our son.

Tears slipped through my lashes. They rolled down my cheeks, splashing his chest. His thumb swiped them away from my eyes, and I lifted my hand to his, holding him in place, eyes still closed. We remained that way until my fingers tightened on his and my body spasmed around him. He cupped my breast, thumb grazing the bud of my nipple, rolling me over the edge. I tumbled down, body folding into his. His arms wrapped around me, holding me against his pounding heart. My pain poured onto him and his poured into me. There was nowhere for it to go, though.

We no longer absorbed each other.

My pulse slowed, pulling the last of the numbness with it. I pulled away from him, again avoiding his gaze. As I moved to disconnect completely, he touched my shoulder.

"Noah, wait."

I focused on my breathing. The levee holding my heart together was close to breaking.

"Please. Come with me." His voice cracked.

Staring down at the trail of soft curls that led to where we connected, I shook my head.

"Noah," he begged in a whisper. "This doesn't have to end."

"I'm not leaving my life so that you can keep leaving us." I lifted my eyes to meet his, my words encasing a final fragile shell around my heart. For the moment, anyway.

"It won't be like that."

I rolled away from him, my body sighing as his warmth left me. Levi could never fill me for long, and he never would. I'd learned to pack the hole he always shot through me, and I wouldn't forget ever again.

"You never choose us," I said, wrapping myself in a silk robe.

He sat up on his elbows. "Why do I have to choose? Why can't I be a doctor and a husband and dad?"

"You can," I told him, cinching the tie around my waist. "You just don't know how. I'm not waiting for you anymore."

Levi stood, bending to collect his clothing. "What are we going to tell Joey?"

Just like that, he was giving up. I closed my eyes. Deep down, a part of me had hoped he'd tell me I was wrong. That he'd fight for us. "There's nothing to tell him," I said. "He knows we're not a family anymore. You never really wanted us, Levi. You just loved the idea of us."

"You never answered my question, Noah," he said.

"Just go," I whispered, wrapping my arms around myself. Every moment with him drilled the pain in deeper.

He sighed, but said nothing. Silence settled into the room, a heavy presence. The air caressed my bare legs as he moved past me. A second later, my bedroom door closed.

A heartbeat after that, the front door closed.

❄ 24 ❄

LEVI

The stairs seemed to go on forever, my legs as heavy as the muscle beating inside of my chest. I only knew it was still beating because of the pain.

I was a doctor. I knew that a metaphorically broken heart couldn't hurt. There was no other way to explain the weighted ache that had settled into its center, though.

She didn't say she loved me. The realization played over and over in my head, a loop that my brain seemed to almost sadistically enjoy. Each rewind brought fresh pain, a sensation that I felt deeper than any muscle or body tissue. The first time she'd left me, I'd been too numb. I hadn't seen it coming, so I spent most of our separation in shock. This time, I'd been caught by surprise again, but there was a fundamental difference.

I'd changed.

Or so I'd thought.

Throughout the past few weeks, I thought I'd learned what it truly meant to be a husband and father. What it meant to love them. To love her. I hadn't even seen the tip of the iceberg, though. What I thought was an excellent decision for my family had been the killing blow.

There was nothing I could do, either.

No amount of repair could fix the damage. I couldn't salvage our relationship with transfusion or time. I'd hurt her again.

And she'd hurt me.

Stepping into my quiet apartment, I went straight to the kitchen for a beer. I'd never been much of a drinker, but it was the only anesthesia I had at hand. Not that it would do much.

The best thing I could do was take the job. It was time to move on. I had no idea what I'd do about custody—if she'd even let me see Joey. That might be another bloody battle. I couldn't imagine her letting him stay with me across the country. We'd already hurt each other in so many ways. There had to be an end to it.

Maybe there could be.

My presence in their lives seemed to be the common denominator. No matter how much it stung that Noah didn't love me, the truth remained that I had a problem, and its name was workaholism.

Knowing that didn't make it any easier. There was no switch that I could just shut off. I would never wake up one day, suddenly less committed to my patients. No matter how much I wanted to prioritize my family, no matter how much I loved them, I could never walk away from medicine. It was as much a part of me as writing was a part of Noah.

She and I might never work. Maybe it was time to let the dream die.

I rubbed my face with a hand. Even though she'd told me to go, I didn't want to walk away. I couldn't leave my family any more than I could leave a patient on the table.

I couldn't take the job.

The salary and benefits didn't matter if I had no one to share them with. There was no one and nothing else in the world I wanted more than Noah and Joey. I was at a stalemate.

I chucked the beer cap into the sink and leaned against the counter, pressing the palms of my hands into its edge. She'd made the choice for me, cutting me out of the conversation altogether when she told me to go. When she refused to answer my question.

I couldn't take the job, but I would. I had to. There was nothing left for me on the East Coast. Not if I couldn't be with my family.

One week. I could make it for another five days. In the morning, I'd give my notice at Yale. I'd spend as much of my down time with Joey as possible. Hell, I was already forgoing two weeks' notice. I could resign immediately. It'd be a blemish on my record but with Stanford on my resume, I'd more than recover.

Recover.

The reminder jarred me out of my grief-driven haze. I had patients who were relying on me. I couldn't up and leave them. Not the three-year-old little boy who'd been born with an autoimmune kidney disease and relied on me to take care of him. His mother was fucking Wonder Woman, but she'd told me I was the only urologist she trusted. I couldn't just flee the state when I had people like them counting on me.

Pouring the rest of the beer down the drain, I tried to get my head together. Somehow, I'd work things out with Noah so that I could continue making an effort to spend time with Joey. No matter how many times we'd hurt each other, she knew how much I loved him. If I stayed, I'd be showing both of them exactly how much.

Noah and I were through. That was an absolute. She'd made it crystal clear, and I had to respect her decision. That didn't mean I couldn't make my own decisions, though.

Calling my own shots did nothing to ease the cracking sensation in my chest, but it at least made me feel like I had a bit more control over the situation. In the morning, I'd call Dr. Sheth and let her know that I couldn't take the position. Then I'd do my damnedest to salvage my relationship with my son. Things with Noah were well and truly over, and I needed to accept it. I'd never walk away from Joey, though. All I could do was hope that he'd meet me halfway and that, in time, Noah and I could be co-parents.

❦ 25 ❧

NOAH

Brynn and I had planned most of our parents' anniversary party through texts over the past few months. The night before, though, we got together to make the decorations. We really only needed to paint the lantern candle holders to make them look weathered, but I'd never complained about more sister time. So I packed up Joey, tucked him in on an air mattress in Brynn's office, and sat on her living room floor.

Decorations littered the carpet: faux pine boughs, pine scented jar candles from Yankee Candle, and instant cameras for guests to take pictures with. Brynn sat with her back against the bottom of the couch, her iPad balanced on her knees.

"I found this pic of Tahoe at sunset," she said, holding the tablet up for me to see. "I thought I'd try to paint the scene on canvas."

"That's ambitious of you." I ran a fingertip along the stiff fabric pine needles.

"You wanna try?"

I shook my head.

"All right then. Have you ever done this before?" She nodded to the paint and lanterns.

I shook my head again. Brynn had always been the crafty one. Every single one of my Pinterest projects ended in tears, so I'd stopped trying. My results were always far from failures and more like abominations. I usually had fun trying, though—aside from the crying.

Brynn held up a lantern and a flat paintbrush, explaining how I was going to paint it "dry," then use sandpaper after it dried to make it look old.

I frowned, but took the white paint brush from her.

"Don't worry about the rug," she said. "I found a steam cleaner on Facebook for dirt cheap."

While I weathered the lanterns, Brynn bent the boughs into circles, which would go around the lanterns. At the hall, we'd put them on tables and add the scented candles. Our goal was to make the room smell elegantly like the tall pine trees that surrounded the lake.

After about twenty minutes of quiet concentration, Brynn broke the silence. "I talked to Mom the other day."

I gripped the brush, my strokes lengthening. "And?"

"She says you never answer her texts."

Sighing, I laid the brush across the plastic I'd pulled off one of the lanterns. "Do we have to do this right now?"

"She's just concerned."

"Concerned," I echoed.

"Yes, Noah," my sister said.

"You don't get it, *Brynn*. You've always had the easier relationship with her."

"That's because I've always just accepted her for the mother she is."

"Which is to say, not much of one at all."

Brynn scoffed. "She didn't leave us, Noah. She's always been in our lives."

"Except when she's at the hospital," I said. "Let's not forget how when she was at home, she always pushed us hard."

"Because she wanted us to have good lives!" Brynn pointed a pine bough at me. "She didn't want us to just settle."

"No, of course not," I said. "How could we *just* be teachers when we should've been doctors?"

Rolling her eyes, Brynn stood. "She never said she wanted us to be doctors."

"She never said she was proud of us for being teachers, either. She wasn't around, Brynn. I know you're a few years younger than me and don't remember everything the same, but she wasn't. She was always so cold and judgmental. Every step I took was wrong. *Is* wrong," I amended.

"I'm getting snacks." Brynn turned on her heel and marched into the kitchen.

I sighed. Sometimes it felt like my sister and I had completely different relationships with our mother. Where Brynn was quick to defend her, I was sure to scrutinize our mother's scrutiny.

Standing, I abandoned my project and joined my sister in the kitchen.

"You know what Mom said to me when I told her Levi and I were buying a house?" I asked, leaning against the counter.

Head bent, Brynn stared down at the blondies she arranged on a plate.

"She asked me why. She didn't even congratulate me. She grilled me about why on Earth I'd stay in Connecticut. Not once has that woman ever told me she's proud of me."

My sister's shoulders sank. "I know you have a tough relationship with Mom," she said, "but why not just let it go?"

"Because!" I yanked my phone out of the back pocket of my jeans. Scrolling through my texts, I pulled her last few up. "'Dad says you moved in with Levi. Have you lost your mind?' And: 'Are you sleeping with him? I thought you were focusing on your career.' Then there's this one: 'I'm glad that's all over with now.'" I slapped my phone down on the counter. "Mom doesn't give you a hard time because you're not even seeing anyone. Just wait."

Brynn lifted her head, her eyes meeting mine. "I wonder if bringing Alex to the party isn't the best idea, then."

"The pizza delivery guy?"

She nodded.

"You'd better prepare yourself, then. 'He delivers pizza? Oh Brynn,'" I said in my best impression of our mother. "'That's hardly even a career.'"

She laughed ruefully. "Okay, I get it now."

"It's not even really Levi that's the issue," I said. "She adores him. I think she wishes he was her child instead of us. It's just that in her eyes, unless you're a surgeon, you're nobody. Just look at what Dad's had to put up with."

"They're still married, though," she said, voice soft.

"Yeah. I guess they are." Bumping my hip against hers, I nodded to the blondies. "Come on. Let's get back to work."

❦

I HATED ALL-NIGHTERS. THEY WEREN'T MY FORTE IN COLLEGE, and I would've made a terrible surgeon. Even though Brynn and I called it a night around one in the morning, I still woke up feeling as if I hadn't slept. Still, I got Joey dressed in his royal blue suit—the color of the Tahoe sky at night. I put on my long-sleeved, knee-length dress in the same color, admiring the way it hugged my curves. Brynn had the same dress, just in emerald green.

"Eggo time," I called to Joey.

"It's a go then!" he shouted, careening through Brynn's and sliding to a stop at my feet. "It's party time!"

Brynn and I exchanged grins. "Let's go get that cake," I told Joey.

"See you at the hall," my sister said.

I drove to Elli's, my thoughts consumed with Levi. A week before, I would've asked him to be my date. Sure, it would've been awkward at first, but he'd always been a good buffer between my mother and me. I'd made my decision, though.

There was no going back.

A few minutes later, I parked in front of the bakery. "Get out on the sidewalk side, I told Joey as I slowly opened my door. In the past year, two business owners had been struck and killed while getting into their cars. I could just see the headline: TEACHER RUN DOWN. Or worse: TEACHER'S SON STRUCK BY SPEEDING DRIVER. Traffic on Main Street was slow, though, so I hustled out and joined my son on the sidewalk.

"Can I hold the door?" he asked, already running to open it for me.

My lips spread into a warm smile. Somehow I'd created, birthed, and raised the most perfect human being—not to mention adorable. The dark blue really suited him.

"Why thank you." I slipped through, holding the top of the door so he could run in after me. Bells on top of the door chimed, announcing our arrival.

Joey bounded up to the counter, where a silver-haired young woman greeted him. I'd never understand the sudden trend to make perfectly healthy hair gray, but I'd never claimed to be hip, either.

"What's the name on the order?" she asked, glancing from Joey to me.

"It should be Clarke," I said. "Probably under Brynn."

Nodding, the woman turned toward the back of the store. "I'll go check our cooler." She tossed Joey a wink over her shoulder, then strolled away.

"She looks like a fairy," Joey said in awe. "You should do your hair like hers, Momma."

"Ha." I touched my hair. I'd dyed the few natural gray hairs that stubbornly poked through just a couple days earlier.

A moment later, the silver-haired woman emerged carrying a tall box on top of a shorter box. She gently set them on the counter, then opened the taller box. "A two-tier white frosted cake, with edible forest flora," she said, turning it so we could see the realistic looking grass, flower buds, and pine cones.

"That's incredible," I breathed. I knew Elli's was good—it'd been around for decades—but the cake took things to a whole new level.

"Thank you," she chirped. "My business partner and I recently hired a cake artist. She's ridiculous."

"I'll say." No matter how complicated my relationship with my mother was, one thing was for sure: the party would be spectacular.

"This is the base," the woman said, opening the other box to reveal a thick but flat tree stump. "It's not edible, though." Joey giggled, and she closed the boxes again. "I'm Char," she said as she handed him a business card. "Please let us know if we can do anything for you and your next event."

"Thank you," I told her, meaning it.

With the cake in my possession, I hurried to the hall. It was at the Wolcott Lions Club, and the last place I would've ever thought to hold an elegant party at. A friend of mine from work got married there, though—back when Levi and I were still married, before Joey was born. The grounds were beautiful and the hall itself was, too. In summer, the flowers, trees, and bridge over the pond formed the perfect backdrops for photos.

I hadn't been back since.

I let Joey lead the way inside, watching him absorb the place through fresh eyes while I swam through memories. How Levi twirled me around the makeshift dance floor. How we took our drinks outside and walked to the other end of the property, hiding out under the stars. How, later on that night, Joey was probably conceived.

It was yet another place where a piece of our history lived. Where it remained forever, while he saved lives on the other side of the country without a single thought for Joey and me.

"Tibby! Pop!" Joey called, putting the box that held the base on a table and running toward my parents.

My mother touched his cheek. "How did you like *Johns Hopkins Textbook of Cardiothoracic Surgery*?" she asked.

He hesitated, glancing back at me.

"Oh," my mother said, straightening. Her eyes crystallized as she took in my presence. "Wouldn't want another surgeon in the family, now would we?"

"Hello, Mother." Resisting the urge to set down the cake and cross my arms, I called Joey back over. "Come on, Joey kangaroo. We've gotta bring these to the kitchen."

"No Levi?" my mother asked as Joey retrieved the base.

"Tib," my dad said, placing a hand on her arm, "that's not—"

"Oh." She waved a hand. "I just thought, considering you're back together, you'd bring him along. I'd love to see my son-in-law."

Mouth dropping open, I glanced around for my son, hoping he hadn't heard. He stood only a few paces away, though, his eyebrows pinched together.

"You and Daddy are back together?" he asked, his little voice bright with hope.

"*No*," I said. "Nan just means because Daddy lives upstairs."

"So he's coming to the party?" he asked. His eyes sought mine.

"No," I repeated, my voice more gentle this time. Confusion continued to flick across his face, though, mirroring in his eyes.

"What an odd arrangement that all was," my mother said.

I shot a glare at my father. I'd sent him *one* text, letting him know that Levi was leaving. I should've reminded him not to say anything to her. I should've known better.

"Tibby." Dad looped his arm through hers, tugging. "Let's go say hello to the Ruckers."

She stood rooted in place, though. "I really don't understand. How could you just let him go?"

I wanted to close my eyes. To take deep, long breaths and count to ten. I didn't have that luxury, though. Not with Joey's brown eyes bouncing back and forth between his Nan and me.

"You don't have to understand, Mother," I said, keeping my voice as low as possible.

"Maybe I would, if you answered my texts."

"Honey," my dad said, again attempting to lead her away. Not my mother, though. She'd never be led, and she'd never let anyone forget it.

"Whose idea was it to break your family apart? His? Because it's unacceptable."

"Momma?" Joey asked, his eyes as big as saucers.

Tears stung my own eyes. I should've known better. I should've picked up my phone and taken twenty minutes out of my day to make sure she understood not to bring Levi up around my son.

"It was mine," I snapped, setting the cake down. "Put the base on the table, honey," I told Joey. I wheeled on my mother. "I forgot to stop by the house and feed the dog. Let's go." Taking Joey's hand, I led him toward the door.

"We got a dog?" he asked.

I sighed. Add that to the list of things I needed to explain.

❧ 26 ❦

LEVI

I pulled into Veterans Memorial Park, heart already racing as I parked next to Theo. It happened sometimes, a sort of pre-run adrenaline boost. The way I felt, though, I could've ran to the park rather than driven. Not wanting to waste another minute, I got out.

I needed to run off the feelings consuming me.

Theo stood by the trunk of his car, stretching to Staind's *Break the Cycle* album. The tinny sound through his earbuds reached me even a few feet away.

"Taking it back," I shouted, jogging in place.

He pulled them out of his ears, the music fading a moment later. "Back to when they were good."

"I heard Aaron Lewis did a country album a few years ago." I shook my head.

"Which is a damn shame." Theo straightened, rising to his full height. "You ready?"

"Are you?" Before he could respond, I took off.

The park was huge, with multiple playing fields and paved paths all the way around. It was a runner's paradise. Not only did it have soccer fields, trails, and a basketball court, but it also had a huge playground. Up until recently, I hadn't bothered to check out that side of the park. Joey and I came a couple of times during spring break, though.

I hoped it wouldn't be the last time.

"Dude, hold up," Theo called from behind me.

Ordinarily, I would've put on a shit eating grin and hassled him for being too pokey—especially considering his legs were longer than mine. Instead, I pushed myself faster, reveling in the way the impact from my feet hitting the ground sprang up along my legs. Each breath of air burned my lungs, slowly building to the runners' high I chased every time I hit the pavement.

"Damn," Theo said, finally pulling up alongside me. He barely kept pace. "You all right?"

I'd have to slow down to talk. Sucking in more air, I sped on, leaving Theo in the dust again.

"Okay," he called. "I'll just go and get the first aid kit. You're gonna end up with a nasty scrape, dude."

When I glanced over my shoulder, he was gone. Slowing, I took deep breaths. He was right. It wasn't worth getting hurt. Turning around, I jogged back to our cars.

Theo leaned against the Tesla. Two Powerades sat on the roof.

"Dude, get those off of there." I glared at him.

"It won't hurt nothing." He tossed one my way. I caught it with one hand. "You know, maybe you could've been an athlete," he said. "You've got good reflexes."

"Surgeon's hands." I joined him, downing half the Powerade in just a few gulps.

"Wanna tell me why you're trying to collapse a lung and break a leg?"

"Not really."

He eyed me while I finished the rest of the bottle. "So everything is great, then?"

"Yeah." I tapped the bottle against the palm of my hand. "Just great."

"Just spit it out so we can run, man."

Exhaling, I sagged against the Tesla. "I didn't take the job."

"Clearly."

"I didn't want to go without her, man. Or Joey. I might've lost my mind, though."

"Oh, you've definitely lost it," he assured me. "For good reason, though. What are you gonna do now?"

I craned my neck. "What do you mean?"

Theo scoffed. "I mean, what are you gonna do now? Noah's here, you're here. What's the game plan?"

"There isn't one. She doesn't want anything to do with me." I thought of the way she'd moved against me that night, her hands fisting the sheets rather than resting on my chest, her eyes closed instead of looking into mine. "It's over."

"So that's it, then? No career advancement, no wife? You're just giving up?"

"I'm not giving up. I'm still working at Yale. I still have Joey." Sort of. I had no idea how he was going to take the news. We hadn't exactly told him we were back together, but of course he'd notice that we weren't sharing dinner anymore. I massaged my forehead.

"So you're completely happy being an attending at Yale for the rest of your life?"

I frowned. "What kind of question is that? Being a surgeon was my dream."

Theo nodded, his brown eyes watching me knowingly. "Uh-huh. Basketball used to be my dream, you know."

"And then you aged out. It happens. You're a coach now. Your high school kids love you, man."

He lifted his eyebrows. "Yup. Plans and dreams change. You've got to see the bigger picture."

"I think the bigger picture's changed for me, too, Theo," I said. "I thought it was Noah, having a family. Now I think it's just family—Joey and me. If I could spend every day the way we spent spring break, I'd die happy."

"Well," Theo said, pushing off the Tesla. He jogged in place. "Not completely happy. Admit it, man. Noah is your bigger picture. Noah, Joey, and whatever comes next."

This time, he took off before I could respond.

27

NOAH

I blinked against the morning light, my eyeballs swollen and heavy. I'd slept maybe twenty minutes total. Every time I thought I'd emptied myself completely, I remembered how Levi disappeared without a word. The look on Joey's face when I told him that his daddy wasn't coming to breakfast, that I didn't know where he was or when he'd be back. How his little shoulders drooped as his eyes met mine.

"Work?" he'd asked.

"I think so," I'd replied.

Come with me.

As if I could upend my life on a last-minute whim.

Still, the ache in my heart permeated throughout my pores until every last limb in my body dragged as I pulled myself through the motions. I'd made the right decision for my family—for myself, even. My heart, however, insisted that I was wrong.

I'd lived without Levi before, though. I could do it again.

After I left him, routine had been the only thing keeping me together. I knew I should get out of bed and go about my day. Fear kept me clinging to the mattress, though, anxiety clouding what I knew and fortifying my worries. I couldn't face Joey and all of his questions. I'd never made any promises to him about his father and me, but all the same, I knew he'd hoped we'd get back together. I didn't know how to tell him that Levi and I weren't going to get married again.

I didn't even know how to tell him that his daddy was moving across the country for a new job.

Fresh tears slipped down my cheeks. I needed to get myself together, but I desperately wished that I could play sick and hide in bed all day. Joey needed me, though, and so did my students. The school would scramble for a substitute if I called out—especially on a Monday—and I didn't want to do that to them unless I absolutely had to.

There were people who needed me, and I needed people—*my* people. Groping the sheets, I found my phone and powered it back on. No missed calls or texts.

Not that I'd truly expected to hear anything from Levi.

I pressed the first name in my favorites list and waited while the phone rang. Though part of me felt ashamed to admit that I'd failed yet again, I needed someone to lean on. There was no better person than my dad. He'd already be on his way to bring Joey to school for me, but I didn't want to sideswipe him with my problems—and I definitely didn't want Joey to know just yet.

"Mornin', sunshine," he crooned. "I'll be there soon. Everything okay?"

Guilt tugged at me for ruining his happiness. I took a deep breath. "Dad," I said, voice cracking. "I need your help."

He paused. I could almost hear him putting the pieces together. "Of course." His voice was a soft salve on my heart. "I'm still bringing Joey in?"

"Yes." I swallowed. "I just—" Taking a deep breath, I tried to steady myself. It didn't work.

"I'll be there soon," he promised.

With the calvary on his way, I could at least take another tiny step forward. I swung the covers back and slid out of bed.

"Momma!" Joey called from the other side of the door. "It's Eggo time."

I was supposed to reply with "It's a go, then!" Clearing my throat, I prepared to answer him, but the doorbell cut me off. I frowned. My dad never used the bell.

"I'll go see!" Joey's feet hurtled away from my door.

"Wait," I called out, but it was too late. A second later, I heard the front door open.

"Daddy!" Joey's voice floated to me from the front of the apartment.

Dread pitted in my stomach. I couldn't let Levi see me. I sure as hell didn't want to see him so soon. Chewing the inside of my cheek, I peeked at my reflection in my standing mirror.

I looked as bad as I felt. Dark circles underlined my eyes and my complexion was cried-all-night pale.

"Where's Momma?" Levi asked, his voice light.

There was no time to do anything about my appearance. Grabbing my fuzzy bathrobe, I cloaked myself in it as if it could make me disappear. I lifted my chin and turned the door knob.

"What are you doing here?" a smoky voice snapped. A voice I'd know anywhere.

My mother.

"Nan!" Joey crowed. "Everyone's here! Is Pop coming too?"

"Pop was on his way but I was closer," my mother said. "I was already at the hospital."

Levi cleared his throat. "I thought I'd take Joey to school."

My mother laughed, a short, cruel sound. "Over my dead body, young man."

"Nan? That's not nice," Joey chided, an undertone of shock coloring his small voice.

I closed my eyes. I had no choice. I didn't know why my dad let my mom come, but I needed to step out and do damage control. Joey was already confused enough. As I opened my door, though, my mother spoke again.

"You're going to be late," she said. Peering through the crack between the door and the frame, I saw her check her watch and sigh. "You can take him to school," she told Levi, "but I'm calling them in an hour. If he's not there, I'm hunting you down. You are *not* taking my grandson to California!"

I rubbed my temples. I was going to have to have a serious talk with my dad.

"Just to school," Levi promised. As he herded Joey out the door, I caught the beginning of my son's string of questions.

"Why is Nan here? And why did she say we're going to California? Where's Momma?"

The front door closed behind them.

Sagging against the frame, I exhaled.

"You can come out now," my mother said.

Of course she saw me. I tightened the tie of my robe and stepped into the living room. For a moment, we appraised each other. She flicked a gaze at my rumpled hair and bathrobe, wrinkling her nose in disdain. As always, she wore a pencil skirt that fell to just below her knees, with her trademark heels. That morning, her outfit was in shades of brown.

"Your father said you needed help."

Even as an adult, her businesslike tone grated on my nerves. All I'd ever wanted was a real mom, the kind who liked spending time with Brynn and me. Instead, we'd had Dad. Even though he was the warm to my mother's cool and always made time for us, I couldn't help but envy other women my age who had close relationships with their mothers.

Mine was only interested in surgery.

In some ways, I supposed I'd married my mother.

I couldn't talk to her about Levi. Never in a million years would she understand. She'd most likely defend him and come up with a thousand reasons why I should've said yes. She'd make me feel bad for choosing my family.

"Coffee?" I asked, already heading into the kitchen. There was no way I could have that particular conversation without some in my system.

As I expected, she chased after me. "Coffee is bad for you."

"No, Mother," I said sweetly as I popped one of the K-cups into the machine. "No caffeine in my system is bad for *you*." As the Keurig burbled and sputtered, a pang rippled through me. I closed my eyes, recalling the morning Levi brought me the box of Gevalia lattes.

"Do you have a headache?" My mother's soft hand whispered across my forehead.

I jerked my eyes open. In her brown eyes, I saw only concern. "No, Mom. I'm fine."

She steered me into a chair. "You don't look fine." Even though my cup of coffee was done, she grabbed one of Joey's juice cups from the dish rack and filled it with water. "How much water are you drinking?"

I stared at the cup as she set it in front of me. "Well, coffee has water in it."

"Don't be a smartass, Noah Clarke."

"Well, I don't think drinking more water is going to solve my problems, Mother." I rolled my eyes. My dad was a dead man walking.

She tilted her head, elegant honey blonde hair brushing her cheeks. If nothing else, the woman was always impeccably put together. "It'll help rehydrate you," she said, voice gentle.

I blinked.

Sitting across from me, she put a hand on top of mine. Again I couldn't get over how soft her skin was. I couldn't remember the last time she'd touched me. "Your father is great with a lot of things, but he doesn't know how it feels for a woman to have her heart broken."

I didn't know what to say. I brought the cup of water to my lips, drinking it mostly to buy myself time. The woman sitting in front of me wasn't the mother who'd raised me.

"I'm sorry," she said in a near whisper.

I put the cup down. "For what?"

"I became obsessed. Any field is difficult for a woman—especially in my generation—but surgery is ruthlessly misogynistic. Women are supposed to be nurses and clean up the messes that doctors don't want to deal with." She shook her head, as if casting off painful memories. "Anyway, I wasn't the mother I should've been. I was cold and distant, and I'm sorry that Levi is doing the same to you and Joey."

She squeezed my hand, but I felt frozen under her touch. I'd never known that. She'd never told me. Of course, on some level I'd always known my mother was a feminist. Her mother immigrated from Sweden and jumped straight into the second wave women's rights movement in the United States. When my mother said she wanted to be a surgeon, my grandmother told her "Of course you can." I'd never thought about just how hard it'd been for her, though.

All my life, I'd missed her. Maybe she could've been more present in my life, but while I fought for her attention, she fought for respect in a field that actively snubbed women.

Levi didn't have that excuse.

"I've missed so much," my mom said. "You and Brynn . . . and now I'm missing Joey. He flat out asked me what I was doing here." She shook her head, tears shining in her eyes.

She meant it.

All my life, I'd longed for those words. In that moment, I had a choice. I could keep carrying the pain of growing up under her shadow, or I could let it go. I could move forward with an open, soft heart, and let her back in.

The choice was simple for me.

"Mom." Her hand still covered mine. I put my free hand over it and met her gaze. "I forgive you."

"Thank you, honey," she said, squeezing my hand. "I hope I can start being a better mother to you and Brynn, and a better grandmother to Joey. That's not what I'm here for, though." She placed her other hand on top of mine.

My eyebrows knit together.

"Don't act so confused. I'm a cardiologist, a woman, and your mother. If anyone knows how to fix a broken heart, it's me. Now," she asked, withdrawing her hands, "are we playing hooky today? Because I know a fantastic nail artist."

"I don't think so, Mom. The school needs me and I really don't feel like getting a manicure."

She nodded thoughtfully. "They're teenagers," she said after a moment. "They don't need you. You, on the other hand, need a shower."

Routine had saved me the first time I left Levi, but the second time, when it seemed nothing could piece together the shards of my heart, the most unlikely of rescuers came to me.

Rolling my eyes, I stood from my seat. "Fine," I said. I grabbed my coffee and poured in the magic powder that made it chocolatey and foamy before she could stop me. "But I'm drinking this coffee, and whether we leave this house or not, I'm going to drink at least three more cups."

She opened her mouth to argue, but I held up a finger.

"I need my mom right now. Not a doctor. Okay?"

She nodded.

Satisfied, I traipsed to my bedroom. I couldn't make Levi stay and I couldn't revive my marriage, but I could fix my relationship with my mom. That would have to be enough.

❧ 28 ❧

LEVI

I closed the door to the classroom, leaving Joey safely at his desk. Being back in Stems and Ivy was weird. The school was where I'd fallen in love with science, in both its simplicity and complexity. If you did X, you were supposed to get Y, but a thousand different variables could change the outcome. It'd prepared me for being a doctor, but it'd also prepared me for life.

Nothing at Stems and Ivy had changed since I graduated. The halls still smelled like lemon polish and old books. I walked out of the science wing, running my hands along carved wooden bannisters, remembering a time when I ran through these halls with my friends. So many of my memories were tied all over the state. For better or worse, Connecticut was my home—and so were Noah and Joey.

I just hoped I wasn't too late in realizing that.

Outside, I dialed Dr. Sheth's number. She answered on the third ring. "Good morning, Dr. Wester."

I grimaced. I'd forgotten about the time difference. "I woke you. I'm sorry."

She laughed. "I'm a surgeon. We don't sleep. You *are* calling early, though. I hope you're not declining my offer."

"Sorry for that, too," I said. "I really appreciate your generous offer, and I'm flattered—and a little surprised—by Dr. Combies's recommendation. I can't accept, though. My . . ." I hesitated, not sure if I could refer to Noah and Joey as my family. Joey was still my son, though, which made Noah family by extension—no matter what.

"It's all right," Dr. Sheth soothed. "I know it's a lot to ask, hence the tempting package."

"I just don't want to leave your patients stuck."

"Oh, don't worry, Dr. Wester. That's for me to figure out. Really, it's for the bBoard to decide. I just wanted to sooth the blow of my sudden departure—which is also not your problem."

"Yeah," I said, thinking of my own patients, "I understand."

"Indeed," she replied. "It's hard, isn't it? Juggling our careers with our families, I mean."

"It is." I paced in front of the Tesla.

"Unless you're a surgeon, you can never understand the war we wage within ourselves. Duty to ethics, duty to our patients, duty to our families. And don't get me started on the healthcare system that complicates the hell out of everything." She laughed.

I chuckled too. "Dr. Sheth, can I ask you how you balance work and family?"

She sighed. "I don't. No surgeon does, I think. It's a selfish profession, which is why I had to make a choice. That's all our lives come down to: this or that; medication or surgery; patients or family. The world needs good surgeons, but our families also need us. All we can do is make the best choices for ourselves."

"That's really eloquent, for a surgeon," I ribbed gently.

She laughed again. "I think I would like working with you, Dr. Wester. You're one of the good ones. You'll figure it out. Ah—I've got a 911 page. Take care, doctor."

I leaned against the Tesla, tapping my phone against the palm of my hand. Declining Stanford's offer was the right thing to do. I knew it deep down in my gut and in my heart. I just didn't know what the next step was.

Even though I was staying in Connecticut, I was still a surgeon. I was still choosing medicine over my family. No matter how hard I tried to be present, there would always be 911 pages.

Unless I left surgery completely.

I tried picturing myself working in a private practice, treating children for strep and colds. I saw myself wearing the white coat and standing in front of the exam table, but the room around it was blurry. The only place I wanted to be was in an O.R., scalpel in my hand.

If I had any chance with Joey, though, I needed to let that dream die. Strip away the parts that made me a surgeon. Without those parts, though, I didn't know who I was. Surely not just a father. I hadn't gone to medical school and completed a surgical internship, residency, and fellowship only to throw it all away. As much as I wanted to be the kind of father who did that sort of thing, I wasn't that guy. Before Noah and Joey, I'd had a dream. I'd been born a healer. I couldn't just walk away from that.

No more than I could walk away from Joey.

Rubbing my temples, I massaged away the throbbing. I didn't know how to be a father and a surgeon. The movies and TV shows made it all seem so easy: get a nanny for the day to day things, then get home for evenings and bedtime. It didn't work that way, though. I could schedule all of my surgeries before 6:00 p.m., but I couldn't change the fact that I still had to be on call. I had a duty to both the hospital and my patients.

I tapped the bottom of my fist against the trunk of the Tesla. Going around in circles thinking was getting me nowhere. All I could do was my best, just like Dr. Sheth said. I needed to accept that I'd have to keep finding ways to work around the O.R.

I just hoped that my best would be enough for Joey, that in time, he could accept it, too. That he could accept *me*.

It was a lot to ask of a six-year-old, though.

MAY

❧ 29 ❧

NOAH

Not even the warmth of spring could thaw the hard edges of my heart, but I tried to let it in, anyway. The end of the grad school term came quickly, and I found myself with an abundance of free time. It was funny how time worked. It was easy to stretch every minute, harder to sit in the stillness. Especially in my own classroom.

Toward the end of the school year, I always did a marathon of movies adapted from books. It was impossible to keep my teenagers focused on writing essays with college deadlines and prom looming, so the movies were a compromise. In the dark of the classroom, though, with *Twilight* on the TV screen, my mind wandered.

I had yet to finish my own book. I didn't even know what I was writing anymore. What started off as a suspense about teens fighting Nazis had turned into a sort of character sketch of a broken family. I'd have to scrap the entire manuscript and start over with intent. I just didn't know what my intentions were.

I sure as hell couldn't call myself a writer when I wasn't even writing anymore. All I could think about was Levi, and how I'd would've things completely differently. How I'd walk the other way when Pamela first introduced us. I'd turn my head when he leaned in for our first kiss. I'd keep both my dorm room and my heart locked tightly.

I wouldn't have Joey, though, and I couldn't imagine life without him. My heart had reached a stalemate, it seemed. All because Levi hadn't left.

He'd stayed.

The room erupted into embarrassed laughter as Bella and Edward kissed for the first time. Ironically, none of my students shied away from making out in the halls. It was funny, how falling in love blinded you to your own environment. I'd let myself think that Levi had changed when he really hadn't.

Yet, he'd stayed.

I didn't know what it meant. He hadn't come to me with some grand proclamation and promises. Throughout the past few weeks, he'd hardly paid attention to me at all. He knocked on my door at random to bring Joey to school. He texted me on late afternoons asking if Joey could come upstairs for dinner. He even took Joey overnight on school nights, even if he had surgery in the morning. Not once had he brought up California again, though.

I didn't know what it meant.

Not for me, anyway.

Instead of trying to figure it out, I spent those empty minutes on my novel. Or I should have. Despite what my heart knew, my head had other plans, going over and over every little text and glance he sent my way, trying to read between the lines.

My students groaned collectively. I glanced up at the screen, smirking. For all its cheesiness, there was something about The Twilight Saga that made it an instant cult classic. Teens related to it because they could put themselves in the characters' shoes. It was too bad that my own characters' shoes were all over the damn place.

After dismissal, I hurried home. One of the other good things about movie marathons was less work to grade. I had a good hour before my dad brought Joey home, and I needed to spend those sixty minutes on my book. Or else all of the time and student loans I was pouring into my degree would be for nothing.

As I pulled into the driveway, though, Pamela's car slid in beside mine.

I got out of the car, unable to keep the concern from my face. Pamela never showed up at my house in the middle of the day. Not since those post-college days when we didn't have jobs yet.

"What's up?" I called as she got out of her car.

She held up a rose gold gift bag. "I've got something for you. Can we go inside?"

"Sure," I said, my confusion deepening. It wasn't my birthday. Unlocking the door, I ushered her inside. The apartment was quiet, the afternoon sunlight glowing throughout the rooms. I hung up my jacket, kicked off my shoes, and plopped down on the couch. Even though I'd been watching movies all day, it felt good to sit somewhere cushioned.

Pamela joined me, tucking her legs underneath her.

"No more T-shirt dresses?" I asked, lips curling. "It's actually warm enough to wear them now."

"Ha, ha," she said. "No, I . . . Well, just open the bag." She set it in my lap.

"Don't tell me," I said, picking it up and testing its weight. It was light. "You're giving me your T-shirt dress collection."

"Close." Grabbing a throw pillow, she tucked it behind her back.

I pulled the cream tissue paper from the bag, dropping each sheet at my feet. Inside lay a carefully folded white T-shirt. "I knew it," I said.

"Just pull it out." Pamela leaned forward, anticipation thrumming through her.

"Is that what you tell Theo?" I smirked.

She swatted at me. "Not anymore. Look at your damn shirt!" Pink tinged her cheeks. Her eyes shone with excitement.

I lifted the shirt from the bag by its sleeves. It unfolded, revealing a single word in delicate black calligraphy: *The Auntourage.*

"Aunt . . . our . . . ?" I felt like a pre-school student sounding out a new word.

Pamela rolled her eyes. "Aunt. Entourage. Auntourage!"

I blinked at her. Her lips spread into a huge, goofy grin. "Oh my god!" I tossed the shirt into the air and gently tackle-hugged her. With my arms wrapped around her, I kissed her forehead. "Pammy! Congratulations!" Tears rolled down my cheeks.

"I'm just a few weeks," she cautioned.

"I know it's scary, but you're going to be okay." I wrapped her hand in mine. "Have you told anyone else yet?"

"You mean Theo? Of course I told him."

"I figured. I mean, am I the only other person who knows?"

She nodded. "I've been holding onto this shirt for a damn long time, hoping to give it to you."

"Hopefully not too long," I joked. "I hope it still fits."

"Don't do that to yourself," she said.

"I just mean, if you've had it since college, I've filled out since then." I spread my arms and wiggled my shoulders. "You're gonna fill out, too."

She shoved me playfully. "Stop."

"You and Theo are gonna make one cute baby."

"We are." After a beat, her brown eyes turned serious. "We'd like to ask you if you'll be our baby's godmother. Not in, like, a stiff religious way. In an in-case-we-die way."

"I don't know, rigor mortis is pretty stiff." I grabbed my "aun-tourage" shirt and refolded it.

"Seriously, Noah."

"Seriously, Pamela. Of course I'll be your baby's fairy godmother or whatever."

"Or whatever." She grinned. "Joey's going to lose his mind when we tell him he's gonna have a baby cousin."

"Either that or he'll lecture you on how they won't *really* be cousins." I rolled my eyes. "He has that literal boy gene that Levi carries so strongly."

"Please, please let me have a girl." Pamela tilted her head at me. "Speaking of Levi, I noticed that he's still in the state. Wanna talk about it?"

"No," I said, drawing out the word. "I wanna get day drunk on wine, but you're knocked up now and ruining all the fun."

"It would be really weird if I celebrated being pregnant by getting drunk."

"Tea, then?" I stood, stretching.

"It's not wine, but I guess it'll suffice." She followed me into the kitchen, where I filled the kettle and set it on the stove.

I sat down at the table, pointedly ignoring my laptop.

"To be clear, you don't want to talk about Levi, even if I told you that Theo said something?"

I sighed. "Especially if Theo said something."

"Okay." She drummed her fingers on the table. "Is it too early to start planning for my baby shower? Or is it still considered uncool to have a gender reveal party?"

"That little bean is your baby. You can celebrate however you want."

"Just as long as I don't get drunk."

"Right." I grinned. "I've missed you. It's been a lot of doom and gloom around here lately."

"Well," she said, "I told you not to go back to school."

I propped my chin in my hands. "Sometimes I feel like I don't know what I'm doing at all."

"Welcome to humanity." Pamela squeezed my shoulder. "Seriously, woman. No one knows what they're doing. They're letting me have a baby, and I can barely keep from spilling food all over my T-shirt dress."

"In that case, you'll do great. Babies are messy." I stood, eyeing the kettle on the stove. "Speaking of, why did you ditch those dresses? They're amazing for pregnant ladies who have to pee every three seconds."

"I don't need them anymore."

"What do you mean?" Just as the kettle started to whistle, I shut off the burner and moved it to a cool one. "They grow with you and everything."

"They're also easy access."

I turned to face her, blinking.

Her expression remained innocent.

Shaking my head, I poured our tea. "You're too much, Pamela."

"Well," she said, accepting the mug I handed to her, "it worked, didn't it?"

❦

I INVITED PAMELA TO STAY FOR DINNER, BUT SHE WANTED TO get home to Theo. It made sense. They were expanding their family, going from a couple to a trio. For the next nine months, she'd be both treasuring that quiet time and anticipating the birth of her child. Once upon a time, I'd been in her shoes.

I threw together spaghetti and called Joey to dinner. Once he was in bed after, I hoped to tackle the blank page and blinking cursor that kept taunting me, getting words down for once and for all.

Joey shuffled into the kitchen, hands deep in the pockets of a pair of child-sized scrubs I'd never seen before. He hopped up into a chair and scrunched his face at his plate.

"What?" I asked, twirling spaghetti around my fork.

He shrugged.

"You don't like spaghetti anymore?" I took a big bite. It was delicious. There was something about a hot plate of spaghetti, meatballs, and sausage that always made me feel better—even if it wasn't the healthiest meal.

"No," he mumbled.

"So what's wrong?"

He shrugged again.

Inhaling through my nose, I reigned in my impulse, which was to call him by his full name and tell him to just eat. I opted for a different tactic. "Where'd those scrubs come from?"

"Daddy," he replied. "They have Minions, too. They were sold out, though."

"Oh." I put my fork down. "Are you worried you'll get sauce on them? I know how to get stains out of scrubs, you know."

"I know." He stared down at his plate.

"Your dad used to come home with some wicked stains," I said.

"It's just . . ." Joey sighed.

"You can tell me." I folded my hands in my lap.

One of his eyebrows twitched.

I frowned. "Are you worried you're going to hurt my feelings?"

He bowed his head.

"Honey . . ." I glanced around the kitchen, as if maybe the right words would appear on the dry erase board I wrote grocery lists on. "It's okay. Whatever it is, you can tell me."

Joey sighed again. "It's just that Daddy's making spaghetti with stewed tomatoes." Lifting his eyes, he met my gaze.

"So you want to eat upstairs."

"Yes. If that's okay?"

I nodded. "Of course it's okay. All you have to do is ask."

He scooted his chair back and hurried out of the apartment as if I'd tried making him eat eyeballs.

I picked up my fork again. It wasn't personal. I knew that. Joey liked spending time with Levi—and that was how things should be. Still, it stung. He'd always loved my sauce and meatballs. Even though I had less free time, I made sure I put together a huge pot at the beginning of every month, freezing portions in containers so that homemade spaghetti sauce night never died.

Yet suddenly Levi did it better, and it stung. Not because Joey ran upstairs, but because I couldn't go with him.

❧ 30 ❧

LEVI

As I walked across the Marshall's parking lot with Joey's hand in mine, it dawned on me that I'd never ran around with him before. The whole time Noah and I were married, she took care of errands, Joey by her side. I couldn't think of a single time I'd so much as gone grocery shopping with him.

The old fashioned accordion doors slid aside as we approached, squeaking reproachfully.

"Should we grab a cart, Daddy?" he asked, looking up at me.

"Probably." *Please*, I prayed silently, even though I didn't believe in any higher power. *Please let him see that I'm trying.* "Uncle Theo and Auntie Pamela are meeting us, but something tells me we're going to need two carts."

He frowned. "So, should I take two carts?"

"No." I chuckled. "We'll let them grab another one. Come on." I held my hands out to him.

Joey lifted a dubious eyebrow.

"Don't you want to ride in the cart?"

Tossing his head back, he laughed loudly. "This is a Marshall's cart, Daddy. Not Costco's."

"Is there some rule about carts that I'm not aware of?" I

grumbled.

"Um, duh." Pamela appeared at my side. Steadying the cart, she waited until Joey hopped onto the metal bar between the front wheels. "Marshall's carts are too small. We're going to need all the room we can get in this baby."

"Duh," Joey said as she wheeled him away.

I turned to Theo. "What the hell just happened?"

He spread his hands. "I think the doctor and the athlete just got schooled. Come on, man. We'll let Pamela handle the baby clothes. I need your opinion on some jewelry."

"Jewelry?" I hurried to follow him inside.

"Yeah," he said over his shoulder. "I need a 'Yeah, I knocked you up' gift for Pamela." He giggled. My giant friend actually giggled.

I grinned, his happiness a palpable and infectious presence.

"Marshall's doesn't have a jewelry department," Pamela called from the women's section.

"Amateurs," Joey added.

"I've never felt more useless in my whole life," Theo said.

"Just wait 'til she actually has the baby." I clapped him on the back. "That tiny little human is going to make you feel completely inept."

The tender way he watched Pamela move through the store made my chest ache. As happy as I was for both of them, I wished it was Noah and me shopping for baby clothes. I tipped my head back, letting my eyes close for a moment. If only there was a surgical procedure that could permanently remove her from my brain, the way I could excise a tumor from a kidney.

A hand slipped into mine. I opened my eyes.

"Come on, Daddy." Joey tugged me forward. Once we were in the baby section, he released my hand and bounded over to the rack where Pamela sifted through tiny onesies.

I joined Theo at an end cap of booties. "Why isn't she shopping with Noah?"

"My wife?" Theo laughed darkly. "Because Noah's at work, and

Pamela wanted to go baby clothes shopping right *now*. Plus," he added, avoiding my gaze, "I think she's trying not to rub it in Noah's face."

"What do you mean?" I picked up an infant's Patriots jersey.

My best friend's eyes widened. "Don't let her see you!" He wrenched the jersey from my hand and buried it within the rack behind him.

"Don't you want your kid to fit in?" I asked.

"Naw. His parents are already traitors to the region." Theo proudly straightened his Miami Dolphins hat.

"More so you. Pamela's a Bears fan. How will that work, by the way?"

"We haven't discussed it yet."

"I don't envy that conversation." I glanced over at my son and his aunt. They were out of earshot. "What did you mean by Pamela not wanting to rub being pregnant in Noah's face?"

Though he towered over me, Theo squirmed like a little boy. "Aw, come on, man. Forget I said anything."

I couldn't, though. The hope pulsing through my veins infiltrated every square inch until it was all I thought about.

A family of four wheeled by us, two toddlers tucked into a double stroller steered by the dad, one of the mom's hands on her very swollen belly. Everywhere I looked, families swarmed the store. If I hadn't been so cocky, I could have my family with me.

Theo sighed. "All right, but listen, you didn't hear this from me."

"Hear what?" I moved farther out of Pamela and Joey's earshot, nodding for him to follow me. "Quit stalling, man. You're killing me."

"It's probably nothing, but Pamela mentioned she got the feeling that Noah's sad."

That was the understatement of the year. Of course Noah was sad. I'd betrayed her trust—again. I bit back the sarcastic response that bounced on my tongue and busied myself by flipping through children's books on a shelf.

"She said Noah got this look on her face when Pamela told her she's pregnant, like a wistful look."

Shrugging, I continued reading the titles.

"I guess they used to have a pregnancy pact before y'all got divorced. Like a running joke, but not."

My head snapped up. "A pregnancy pact? That sounds . . ."

"Just like our wives?" Theo supplied. "I told you, man, it doesn't mean anything."

It did, though. Noah and I talked about having a second child a few times. We never made it to the ditching birth control stage of that particular discussion, but she'd made it very clear that she didn't want Joey to be an only child. She'd grown up with a sister close in age, and she didn't want him to be alone—just like I hadn't wanted him to have divorced parents.

Then she left me.

I scanned the shoppers and racks until my gaze landed on my son and Pamela. Noah and I couldn't give Joey the things we'd wanted to give him, but maybe with a little luck, he and Pamela's kid would be as close as siblings.

As long as I made an effort to stick around, he might have divorced parents, but he'd never be without both of us. He'd never be alone.

One of so very few certainties in life was that it never went as planned. All I could do was my best for the people I loved. For Joey, that meant staying. For Noah, that meant letting her go.

I knew how. It was simple. I just didn't know if I could survive being without her. Physically, I'd be just fine. I'd keep doing what I was already, pushing myself through the everyday motions. Emotionally, though—that was a different story.

Noah was it for me. No one could ever compare. There was no version of the future where I fell in love with someone else and started anew. All I could do was work with the broken family that I had.

Theo clapped my shoulder. "You all right, dude?"

"No," I said, "but I will be."

❧ 31 ❧

NOAH

The clock on my laptop ticked toward midnight, its unblinking display as accusing as the flashing cursor in my word processor. It was a good thing I didn't have any sort of deadline, because I would've been late twenty times over. For some reason, I just couldn't finish my book. Maybe I never would.

I clicked away from the manuscript and opened Safari. My co-workers teased me relentlessly for using it, but for all of its flaws, I couldn't walk away. I liked its simplicity. I liked that I could access the same bookmarks from my iPhone and MacBook Pro. I liked that, when certain websites had too much crap to be printable, I could usually get a nice clean version in Reader View. Maybe I stubbornly clung to something outdated, but it worked for me.

I surfed Pinterest aimlessly, hoping for some inspiration. Usually I found comfort in the writers' memes and writing advice, but it was all the same old stuff: screenshots of writing prompts on Tumblr; plot structures; Stephen King quotes from *On Writing*. On any other night, I'd appreciate those nuggets of advice, but the closer it got to 1:00 a.m., the further I was from getting any actual writing done.

Sighing, I closed the laptop and pushed it away from me. Maybe it was time to give up the ghost. Having a love for reading books didn't give me the right to write them. Teaching literature to teens didn't give me a license to write books for them. Knowing what they really wanted to read about wasn't enough.

None of it was enough.

It was time to accept reality. I wasn't a writer. Going to school for marketing was a waste of time and money. I needed to stay in my lane and teach.

I taught my students to never give up, though. If I quit, I couldn't look into their faces and tell them not to do the same. I'd be a hypocrite. Still, writing was obviously not happening for me.

I opened my laptop, then scrolled back through my story. I'd written a little over 20,000 words, which amounted to about a third to a quarter of a typical novel. My characters resembled shadows more than actual people, moving through the plot aimlessly while things happened to them. As I read through what I had, I used the comments feature to add notes. When I reached the last sentence—which wasn't even complete—I sat back in my seat.

There was nothing salvageable.

The only thing to do was send it to the trash.

Then, I could start fresh.

My finger hovered over the document. If I deleted it, there was no going back. If I kept it, though, it'd hang over me forever.

I dragged it to the trash icon.

The delete sound effect had never felt so satisfying.

Opening a new document, I stretched my neck. My characters needed purpose. Rather than focusing on all of the things I wanted to say, I needed to pick a single message. One of my all-time favorite stories was *Romeo and Juliet*—except for the ending. It'd always seemed so far-fetched to me. Instead of jumping to conclusions and killing themselves, they could've fought. It frustrated me to no end, and the teens I taught the material to felt the same.

Generation Z was all about making the world a better place and fighting for what they believed in.

Fingertips to keys, I shoved away all of my doubts and what I thought I should be saying, and let my heart guide me instead. The girl who took shape on the page had fears and things she desperately wanted. It wasn't just the hero's love, though. She also wanted to stamp out the racial resentment in her city. Even though she held very little power in her hands, she was determined to try, to make her world better even if she lost everything.

To get her happy ending at all personal cost.

By 3:00 a.m., I had character sketches of my protagonists and a very loose plot structure. It was only a small step, but it was more than I'd managed in months. Part of me wanted to stay up and keep going, see how much of a full outline I could get done before I had to go to work. I needed at least a few hours of sleep, though. Besides, the more I wanted to keep going, the more productive I'd be the next time I sat down at the keyboard.

Before I shut down my laptop, I went to my blog dashboard. I'd been keeping track of my slowly crawling word count in a sidebar widget. As much as I hated to delete that progress bar, I needed the symbolic fresh start of a brand new word count meter.

I deleted it in just a few clicks, then added a new widget. The cursor blinked in the project name field, waiting for me to type in the title. I didn't have one yet, though.

Instead, I put in a date—my deadline.

32

Knocking on Noah's door, I took a step back. The spring morning air swirled around my freshly shaved jaw, unseasonably cool—a typical New England dick move. It'd be almost eighty degrees one day, then fifty the next. I hoped Joey had on more than the thin windbreaker he'd worn the day before.

The door opened and Noah blinked at me.

"It's my day to bring him to school," I reminded her.

"Right." She nodded, the ponytail that gathered just at the border of her occipital bone bobbing.

Something about a ponytail midway down the skull always drove me wild. I hadn't seen Noah with one in a long time. I had fond memories of winding that ponytail around my hand, tugging gently as I moved in and out of her.

She cleared her throat, lifting an eyebrow as if she read my thoughts.

Once again, the ache of her absence clamped around me. I'd blown my second chance. Standing on her stoop, reminiscing her was pathetic. I sighed.

"Does he have a warmer jacket?"

"What?" She frowned at me.

"It's chilly," I said.

"Oh." She blinked a few times, then wrapped her sweater tighter around her. Maybe I imagined it, but I swore the lightest touch of a blush whispered across her cheeks.

I wanted to hit myself. Of course I imagined it. Once Noah made up her mind about something, that was it. No way in hell she was thinking about the same thing I was.

She reached up, twisting the ends of her hair around her finger, her gaze absent. In an instant, my throat went dry and every drop of blood in my veins hurtled down into my cock. The rapid rush sent me back a step, a stagger that I might've played off. Luck had other things in mind.

Noah glanced up, shaking herself out of wherever her thoughts had been. "Are you okay?"

Steadying myself, I turned away. My jacket only fell to my hips. I cleared my throat. "Yeah. Just tell Joey I'll be in the car."

"You can come in, you know."

There it was—the olive branch I'd been longing for, along with the slightest hint of yearning. Or maybe I was imagining that, too. It seemed both the weather and my heart were playing tricks on me.

My hospital phone vibrated in my pocket with an incoming text. Without even looking at her, I heard Noah sigh softly. Another moment ruined.

Tugging the phone out, I read the 911 page. A trauma, seven-year-old boy. My shoulders fell. "I'm sorry," I said. "Tell Joey I'm sorry." Without looking back at her, I jumped into the Tesla.

I couldn't stand to see the disappointment on her face.

Not again.

※

AFTER SCRUBBING OUT OF MY EMERGENCY SURGERY, I TOOK THE elevator down to the lobby. Sometimes I liked sitting in the hushed silence there. It was a way of decompressing after having my hands inside a small body. This time, though, there'd be no quiet processing. I had to tell my patient's family that he hadn't made it.

He'd been just a year older than Joey. Even though he looked nothing like my son, it was still Joey's face I saw the entire time I worked on him. In the end, I couldn't save him. The damage was too extensive.

My resident fell into step beside me. She touched my arm, slowing my pace. "Dr. Wester, do you want me to notify the family?"

Crossing my arms, I looked down at my sneakers. I couldn't get the kid's face out of my head. Instead of driving my son to school, I'd tried saving someone else's son. A boy who'd been on his way to school, too, when an exhausted truck driver plowed into his bus.

"Doctor?"

Every time I stepped into that O.R., I missed precious hours with Joey. Time that I might lose at any second, that I could never get back regardless. I couldn't save them all. I knew that. Still, I'd always believed that it was my job to try.

Maybe it wasn't my job anymore.

"Dr. Wester?" my resident asked.

I rubbed at my face. "If you don't mind, Dr. Dean, can you let the family know? I need a moment."

"I understand," she said gently. Patting my arm once more, she resumed the walk to the lobby.

Tears burned my eyes. Blinking them back, I turned and headed away from the death and devastation. Many other families were in that lobby, waiting to hear about their children. The bus hadn't been full, thank goodness, but as far as I knew, most of the passengers were severely injured.

I found myself in the nursery. Wrinkly, pink infants wriggled in their bassinets, their soft coos enveloping me. The nursery was a place of life, one of the few areas in the hospital that didn't depress me. Not so long ago, Joey had been one of those new babies. At the time, I'd thought I could do it all—be a doctor, husband, and father without consequences. Instead, I'd lost the love of my life, and if I wasn't careful, I'd lose Joey, too.

Then I'd only have surgery, and even that felt lost to me. When that boy flatlined, something in me died with him. I didn't want to be the last in line anymore, the last thing standing between a child and life or death.

Stepping into the hall, I pulled my personal phone out of my scrubs pocket. My finger hovered over Dr. Sheth's name. It was a long shot. The odds that she'd know of any job openings were, well, pretty slim. I closed my contacts, frustration and desperation eating at me like acid.

My phone vibrated in my hand. The caller ID flashed a familiar name, a woman who rarely called me, even in the best of times.

Noah's mother.

I swallowed. I couldn't imagine Noah telling her mom about our breakup, but there was only one reason she could be calling.

Dr. Tibby Clarke was about to verbally eviscerate me.

I took a deep breath, gathering strength as I accepted the call. "Hello, Mom," I said smoothly, opting to pretend like everything was fine between her daughter and me.

"Don't 'Mom' me," she said. "You are *not* moving to California."

So much for pretending.

"I'm not," I promised.

"You're damn right," she said.

"Tibby . . ." I pinched the bridge of my nose. Before the divorce, I actually got along with my mother-in-law. I knew from the liner notes Noah shared with me from her childhood that she could be prickly. I didn't have it in me to dodge her barbs, though.

I shouldn't have answered the phone.

"Are you all right?" she asked, her tone changing from brisk to concerned. "You sound upset."

"I need to get out. I just . . ." The words caught in my throat. Balling my hand into a fist, I wrangled my emotions. It wasn't the first time I'd lost a patient. I'd even lost younger children—babies, even. It always sucked, but it didn't usually get to me.

Tibby waited patiently while I took deep breaths.

"I'm sorry," I said. "I lost a patient, and it's hitting me really hard."

"I think we all have those cases," she soothed. "Mine was an elderly woman. I felt so silly. Why should I cry over a woman who'd lived a long life? Yet her death struck a chord with me."

"I can't do this anymore," I confessed. "I miss my son. I love surgery, but I need to be with my family."

"I agree," she said, returning to business. "Which is why I called."

"I'm not leaving," I reminded her. I paced down the hall, glancing into the nursery where all those babies waited to go home with their families.

"I know. One of my fellows is opening a private pediatric practice in New York. It's something new—an autoimmune disease clinic. They're looking for a pediatric urologist, and I recommended you."

I stopped pacing. "Me? Why?"

"Because whether you're married to my daughter or not, you're still a damn good doctor. I recommended you because they would be lucky to have you."

"Thank you," I said. It seemed that, along with my emotions, I'd leaked out all my words.

"And," she added, "now you have no reason to leave. You should be hearing from them soon. I'll text you their contact information. The pay isn't what you're used to," she warned. "You'll be taking quite a cut."

"How much of a cut are we talking?" I asked, head spinning.

"They're offering $110,000. You might be able to talk them into $119. However, they keep standard office hours. You won't work weekends. You'll have much more time with your family."

"Thank you," I said again, incredulous.

"No need. Like I said, it's a win/win for everyone. I've got to run, though. I'm heading into surgery. Good luck, Doctor."

"You too," I told her.

For a while I stared at my phone in my hand. The opportunity I so badly needed was right within my grasp. All I had to do was reach out. I didn't have much experience with autoimmune diseases, though. My mother-in-law's recommendation held a lot of weight, but her fellow more than likely wanted someone more knowledgeable than me.

It was worth a shot, though. If I could talk her fellow into an interview, I could prepare by reading everything about autoimmune diseases that I could get my hands on. Joey wasn't the only nerd in the family who liked reading medical texts.

Taking a deep breath, I opened the text. My finger hovered over the phone number, and I swallowed hard to clear the pressure building in my sinuses.

33

NOAH

"**G**oodnight, Momma," Joey said, throwing his arms around my neck.

I pushed my MacBook off my lap and onto the couch and engulfed him in a hug. "Don't forget to brush your teeth."

"I *know*." He rolled his neck in dramatic protest, eyes bugging out. "I'm not a little kid."

"You aren't," I agreed, "but I'm reminding you anyway."

He froze, his little mouth dropping open.

"What?"

"I forgot my toothbrush at Daddy's!" He bonked his forehead with the heel of his hand.

"So go get it." I reached for my laptop again.

Joey grimaced. "That's . . . not gonna work."

"Joey," I began, infusing my tone with the lightest of warnings. "If you're such a big boy, then you can walk upstairs and get your own toothbrush." From the moment I figured out what my story was about, I'd been pouring every spare second into working on it. I could use the extra few minutes. Not that he needed to know that.

It was supposed to be a parenting moment, after all.

My son looked down, his gaze heavy as he trailed his fingers along the arm of the couch. He sighed.

"Are you still upset with Daddy for not bringing you to school last week?" I asked gently.

His shoulders rose and fell, his lower lip sticking out.

My heart ached for him. It wasn't fair. Levi was always choosing work over us. Well, Joey—we were no longer an us. Logically I knew it wasn't his fault that he'd been paged to an emergency when he was supposed to bring Joey to school, but still. It'd hurt Joey's feelings, and when Joey hurt, I felt the sting too.

As much as I wanted to hug him and assure him that I'd get his toothbrush, we were still in a parenting moment. It was my job to teach him to face his pain. I took a deep breath.

"I know your feelings are hurt, but you can't avoid Daddy forever," I reminded him.

"Just a little bit longer?" he asked in a small voice.

Glancing between my son and my manuscript, I weighed the options. If I made him go, I could snag a few more minutes of focus. Plus there was that whole teaching him to be a direct person thing. His brown eyes bore into mine, pleading.

Shit.

"Joey," I warned.

"Please?" His eyes grew rounder and larger, like freakin' Puss in Boots from *Shrek*.

"Joseph." I sighed. He knew exactly what he was doing, and it was working. I closed the laptop. "Look at me." I lifted his chin. "I'll go get your toothbrush tonight, but while I'm up there, I'm talking to Daddy. The two of you are going to get together and talk about this."

"Okay," he agreed, bounding off to his bedroom.

"Okay?" I asked the empty living room. I'd expected more of an argument. Shrugging, I pulled on sneakers, suiting up for battle. I knew Levi was home. I also knew that he wasn't going to like what I had to say.

He'd made vows to his patients, but he needed to stop breaking promises to his son.

Even if that meant breaking off the rides to school. It'd be better for Joey in the long run. They could plan other activities, like dinners—if Levi stuck to his no surgeries after six rule.

I climbed the stairs, running through each of my points. I wasn't in the mood to argue, and wanted to get the toothbrush and wrap up the conversation as quickly as possible. My words were better spent on my book.

Lifting a hand, I rapped my knuckles on the door twice.

"Come in," came Levi's muffled response.

For a moment, I considered knocking again as if I hadn't heard him, so that he'd come to the door. It'd all be over faster if I didn't go inside. I couldn't tell my son not to run away, though, if I kept playing the avoidance game too. Making a face, I turned the knob and stepped into Levi's apartment.

Tea light candles flickered throughout the living room, their tiny flames casting a glow onto the otherwise dark walls. "Did your power go out?" I called, even then wondering if I should run back downstairs and check on Joey. The hall light in the stairwell was still on, though, and Eisley played softly. Unless Levi's apartment was on a different fuse, he still had power.

I followed the trail of candles into the kitchen. "Why are you sitting in the dark?"

Levi stood from his seat at the table. "I was waiting for you."

"For me?" I crossed my arms. "With your lights off?"

He sighed. "This is my grand gesture, Noah Clarke. Pay attention."

"I'm just here to get Joey's toothbrush."

The corner of his mouth twitched. "Yeah?"

"Because he didn't want to see you, which is why I'm here to talk to you . . ." My voice trailed off.

Joey's easy acceptance of my terms. The candles. My favorite band.

My arms dropped to my sides. "Levi, we can't."

"Just hear me out." He crossed the room to me, cupping my shoulders with those hands. Magic hands that saved lives and brought me over the edge every time they danced across my body. He cleared his throat. "Noah, I know I've let you down. I told you that I'm not leaving you anymore, though, and I meant it. I didn't take the job in California." His eyes held mind, steady and hopeful.

"I know," I said slowly. "I put two and two together when you didn't move out."

"No job, no amount of money is worth risking losing you and Joey."

Holding up a hand, I interrupted him. "You'll always have Joey. He's your son. But Levi, I can't do this anymore. I'd never ask you to leave surgery. I know it's your calling, that something inside of you needs to save people. I love that about you." Tears burned at my eyes, slid down my cheeks. "But I need you *here*. I need to know that you're not going to walk out on me mid-sentence because you've been paged." I swiped the tears away. "I know that's selfish. Believe me, I know."

His grip on my shoulders firmed, the pads of his fingers firing signals through my nerves, igniting my heart. Damn him. Every time he touched me, I forgot all reason. My traitorous body and heart overrode my brain.

I needed to get out of reach.

Taking a step back, I severed the connection. Immediately I could think again.

"You're not selfish," he said, soft words grazing my senses.

I yearned to lean into his touch, to let him wrap those arms around me. The damage between us was so extensive, though. I couldn't keep ignoring the facts. There was no going back.

"I thought surgery was my life," Levi continued. "I was wrong, though, Noah. My life is right here. It's you and Joey. It's always going to be you."

Touching my hair, I looked away, trying not to think about how much easier it'd all be if only he would walk away.

"Just . . ." He sighed. "Just look at the table." He pointed to a manila folder and pen that I hadn't noticed.

The longer I stayed, the more false hope I gave him. "I just came for the toothbrush," I said. My feet, however, remained rooted to the kitchen floor—my body again betraying me.

Might as well get it over with.

I pulled the folder closer to me, then flipped it open with one finger. "Culbertson Autoimmune Clinic and Research?" I ran my fingers across the letterhead.

"Read it out loud."

"'Dear Dr. Wester,'" I read, "'We are pleased to offer you employment at Culbertson Autoimmune Clinic and Research as our pediatric urology specialist.'" Lashes fluttering, I lifted my gaze and met his eyes.

He nodded. "Keep going."

I scanned through the brief offer of employment, then read through the attached contract. "It's signed and dated yesterday."

Catching my hands in his, Levi turned me to face him. "I've already put in my letter of resignation at Yale. In two weeks, I'll start at the clinic. It's nine to five, no weekends. It'll be a long commute, but Noah . . ." His lips trembled. "If you'll have me, I'm here. I'm yours."

My mind reeled. I came upstairs prepared to fight him. Instead, I'd found everything I'd ever wanted. He'd even gone to the trouble to put on Eisley—a band I knew he didn't love, that he'd only tolerated during our marriage on my account.

"Either way," he continued, "I won't be a surgeon anymore. I'll keep my promises to Joey—no matter what happens between us. I'll be here for him. But Noah, I want to be here for you, too."

Frowning, I turned and traipsed into the living room. I all but collapsed into the couch as I struggled to gather my thoughts.

We could only move forward. Levi made the choice I could never ask him to make. The future rested in my hands.

I just needed to take the chance.

❧ 34 ❧

LEVI

Sweat popped out on my forehead as I watched Noah think. I'd played my last card, and I'd botched it all. We were really and truly flatlined.

Instead of leaving, though, she remained seated on the couch. "I really only came for the toothbrush," she said, staring at her hands.

I shoved my hands into my pockets.

"So Joey isn't really mad at you?"

Hope spread through my chest like an ink stain across my white T-shirt. I latched onto it, unable to resist. "He was," I explained. "We talked, though. I told him about the job offer and asked him what he'd think if I took it."

She shook her head, a smile playing on her lips. "He played me."

"He did." Crossing the room, I sat beside her on the couch. "Don't be mad at him for lying, though. I asked him to."

"I'm not mad." She ran her tongue along her upper lip. "It's just a lot to process."

I nodded. "I get that. If you need time, take it."

She lifted her eyes, pinning me. "We're supposed to be divorced," she said softly.

"I know."

"We were supposed to go our separate ways."

"I know," I said again.

Her gaze turned wistful. "I want to trust you."

I waited.

"You make it so hard, though. Then you go and do this." She swallowed. "I don't want you to do this because you think it's what I want."

"I already did it," I reminded her, "but I'm not just doing it for you or Joey. I'm doing it for me." Twining my fingers with hers, I scooted closer on the couch. "That morning I got paged away, I realized I couldn't do it anymore. I don't want to stand at that table, desperately trying to undo damage. I want to tend it before it gets out of control."

Her teeth sunk into her lower lip, her eyes doubtful.

"I know not every patient I've operated on had an autoimmune disease, but a lot of children have kidney diseases because of autoimmunity. We know so little about autoimmune diseases. By pitching in and helping further research, I might be able to do more for my patients. And I'll definitely be with my family."

"What if you wake up one day and realize you made a mistake? What if you miss surgery?" she asked.

"If you say yes," I said, sliding off the couch and dropping to one knee, "I'll have no regrets." Releasing one of her hands, I swept underneath the couch for the little black box. My fingers closed around it and I tugged it free. Then I held it out to her. "I also asked Joey about this."

"Levi," she breathed.

"Noah Clarke, I know this is a lot to take in, but I'm all in. I want you to marry me—again. I can't undo what I've done, but I can be better going forward. I *will* be better, because I don't want to spend another day with these goddamn stairs between us."

Tears streaked down her face, but she smiled through them. "I do hate all of the up and down."

"Say yes," I said, "because I want to put this on your finger and take you to bed."

An eyebrow arched at me. "Oh? Is that how you think this grand gesture of yours is ending?"

"Let's just say I told Joey not to wait up for you."

The laugh that escaped her lips warmed me from the outside in. She covered her mouth with her hands, shaking her head. "You're terrible."

"I'm also out on a limb." I licked my lips.

Exhaling, she lowered her hands. "I'm not getting married again," she said.

I bowed my head. "Well, I can't say I don't know why."

"No." She cupped my chin, lifting it until our eyes met. "I mean *again*. After this. I'm not doing the whole divorce and re-married thing again. This is your last chance, Doc."

"What are you saying?"

"Yes. I'm saying yes."

Hands tingling, I plucked the ring from the box and slid it onto her finger. "I'm not entirely sure I'm not dreaming," I whispered.

"Me either, to be honest."

Leaning forward, I caressed her face. Her eyes fluttered closed as she arched into my touch. Slowly, I touched my lips to hers. She moved against me, her mouth buttery silk. As I parted her lips with mine, she slid down from the couch and into my lap.

"Should I put my hair into a ponytail?" she whispered.

Grinning, I lifted her into my arms as I stood from the floor. "I knew it."

"Where are we going?"

"Downstairs. I plan on spending the night with you, and Joey can't be alone that long."

"You're right," she agreed as I carried her down the stairs. "He needs to wake up to both his parents."

I kicked the door shut behind me. The tea lights would burn

out on their own. I hurried downstairs with Noah in my arms, my heart thumping against my sternum. Once inside her apartment, I slipped into her bedroom. Soon we'd have to consolidate, get rid of the separate apartments. We wouldn't be able to afford building a house on my new salary, and it was far too late to get the old one back, but none of that mattered. The only important thing was the future, and the people that filled it.

My wife and son.

Lowering Noah onto the bed, I cupped the lovely swell of her bottom with both hands. I pulled her all the way to the edge, pressing myself hard against her.

"Let's just try not to traumatize our son," she whispered.

"I'll do my best."

Layer by layer, I peeled and shed the barriers between us until we lay skin to skin. I nestled myself between her folds. Her hands found my shoulders, fingers squeezing gently.

"Shit," I muttered.

"What?"

"Condom." I wished we'd stayed upstairs.

She rolled her eyes at me. "Do you have short-term memory?"

"No. Why?"

"Birth control." She thrust against me, rubbing against my head.

Swallowing, I met her halfway, slipping inside her. "You're so bossy, Mrs. Wester."

"It's still Clarke for now," she reminded me with a smirk.

"You are taking my last name, though, right?"

"Again?" Her center hugged me tightly as I glided in and out of her, those bright sapphire eyes locked on mine.

"Of course, you don't have to," I said quickly. "Your students, for one. That might be confusing. Then there's your book."

"You're too easy."

"Well, duh." I buried myself in her to the hilt. She shuddered around me, each spasm taking me closer.

"Do that again," she said, and we stopped talking.

I folded myself around her, holding her close. Her scent engulfed me, reminding me of our past, the history I'd sold for the high of surgery—but also promising the future ahead of us. When I moved, she rolled with me, and I knew that I'd treasure and honor the second chance I'd been given.

I showed her how much I loved her with tender touches, my forehead to hers, our hearts beating in tandem. I'd show her my presence for the rest of our lives by pulling into the driveway in time for dinner and lounging in bed on the weekends. As I took her over the edge and into the future with me, I sealed the vow by giving her what we both wanted.

We just didn't know it yet.

❦

I WOKE UP THE NEXT MORNING IN NOAH'S BED. SHE LAY ON HER side, those deep ocean eyes locked on mine.

"Good morning." She smiled.

"Shall we fill Joey in?"

Swallowing, she nodded, her eyes glossed with emotion. "I don't think I can wait."

"Me either." I pulled her in for one more kiss, though.

We dressed quickly, then headed down the hall. My heart thumped in my chest. Even though I knew our son longed for us to be together again, my nerves still wound tightly, muscles tense. His approval was the only one that mattered.

Tapping my knuckles lightly on Joey's bedroom door, I exchanged glances with Noah. "Joey," I called. "Can we come in?"

She smiled, her hand on my arm. Her smile and touch should've reassured me, but all I could think of were the what ifs. For the longest time, Joey hadn't let us forget how much he wanted us back together. Still, my nerves wound around my throat, closing off the air from my lungs.

I'd never been so nervous in my life.

"Yes!" our son called.

Noah pushed open the door, tugging me inside. Bright light filtered in through the windows, painting the perfect Sunday morning for a little boy. Joey sat in the middle of his room, all of his action figures out and arranged in the town he liked to set up and play in. He had one in his room upstairs in my apartment, too.

I cleared my throat. "Hey, Joey." As if we'd rehearsed it, I sat on one side of him and Noah sat on the other, moving aside a plastic Happy Meal Barbie. She tucked her legs beneath her.

"Do I have to clean my room?" he asked, eyes darting from the general store he'd made out of cardboard and craft sticks, to Noah's old dollhouse that he'd repainted to look more realistic.

"No, baby." Noah smoothed a lock of his hair from his forehead. "Daddy and I have a question for you." Over his head, her eyes met mine.

I swallowed. "Your Momma and I . . ." I picked up a mini Peter Venkman. It shouldn't be so hard to tell our son we were getting back together. "Joey, do you miss being a family?"

His eyes ricocheted from my face to Noah's. "Momma, you said we already were a family."

She bit her lip. "You're right, I did. We've been a different kind of family, though. Your Daddy and I are wondering . . ."

I cleared my throat again. "We're wondering how you'd feel if we all moved back into one apartment."

"What do you think about Daddy and I getting back together?" Noah asked, re-phrasing the question.

I tapped Peter Venkman against the palm of my hand, my eyes locked on Joey's face.

His forehead wrinkled, his lips flattening while he thought about it. "So you're getting married again?" he asked after a moment.

"I proposed last night, Gnarly Joe."

"Did you vlog it?" he asked.

I chuckled, Noah and I exchanging amused glances over his head. "I didn't. Are you upset that you weren't there?"

His frown deepened. "Well," he began, "a little . . ." His face lit up. "You know how vloggers sometimes have to film more than one take of certain things? Could you maybe do another take?"

Lifting an eyebrow, Noah shrugged.

Want to? I mouthed to her over his head.

Why not? she mouthed back.

I dropped the toy in my hand. I hadn't prepared at all; reliving the moment, with our son present, made it all the more monumental. I passed Joey my phone. He pressed record, indicating that we were rolling with a short nod. Taking Noah's hands in mine, I lifted us both to our feet. Then I bent on one knee. Turning, I reached for Joey, drawing him into my side. With my other hand, I held Noah's. "Noah Clarke, will you do me the honor of being my wife?"

"Again," Joey added.

Tears spilled from her eyes. She nodded, a smile trembling on her lips. "Yes."

The pressure I'd felt in my chest for the past year or so loosened, dissipating altogether. I inhaled as if it was my first breath, using it to climb to my feet. Tipping Noah's chin back, I captured her lips with mine, losing myself in the kiss.

Joey tugged on the hem of my shirt.

Grinning against Noah's mouth, I pulled away. "Yes?"

"Can you guys get married today? Before you change your minds?"

"I'm sorry, baby," Noah said, kneeling in front of him. "I don't think that's gonna happen. We need time to plan and invite people."

Pulling my phone out of my pocket, I Googled town hall hours. I already knew Watertown's was closed on Sundays, but somewhere there had to be one that was open. "Well," I said slowly, holding my phone up for her to see, "Bristol City Hall is open 'til nine tonight."

"I'll be your best man," Joey said, putting each of his small hands in ours. "Do you guys still have your rings?"

An hour later, we stood in Bristol City Hall, Joey in between us as we signed our new marriage license and swore on it. The hall's justice of the peace signed beneath our names, officially making us husband and wife again. He grinned down at Joey.

"It's your line, little man."

My son's face split in the biggest smile I'd ever seen on him. "I now pronounce you husband and wife. You may kiss the bride."

So I did.

EPILOGUE

NOAH

NINE MONTHS LATER

The February cold frosted the living room windows outside, but I fanned myself with a magazine. It figured that I'd be unreasonably hot in the dead of winter. It wasn't my fault, though. I was damn near bursting with baby. Damn Levi. I sat nearly on top of the cracked open window, considering taking advantage of the central air in the new house, winter be damned. We'd been living in it for almost six months but both Levi and I still referred to it as "the new house." When I found out I was pregnant, we tossed aside our plans to keep renting my first floor apartment and went full throttle into home-buying mode.

As if in response to my thoughts, Tierney kicked up into my ribs. "Oof. It isn't nice to beat on your Momma, you know," I warned her.

Levi glanced at me from the floor where he worked on a poster board with Joey. "Need me to help you get her out of your ribs again?"

I groaned in response. On one hand, it was good that she'd

turned. It meant she'd be out of me any day. On the other hand, though, it was a real pain, having those feet so close to my ribs. Both Levi and Joey kept reminding me that she was in the anterior position—a habit that had me rolling my eyes every single time. They'd shown me diagrams of babies in various birth positions. It was too bad I couldn't pick, because I would've chosen the posterior head-down position, putting those little feet belly-side. I had enough padding there. My belly could take a beating.

My ribs, on the other hand . . .

"Yes, please," I begged my husband. Tierney already proved to be one headstrong little girl. When I'd gotten pregnant, I was on birth control. Turns out that one percent margin of error was pretty hefty when it failed.

Levi hopped up from the floor and joined me on the couch. Gently, he used his hands to pull our daughter's feet out of my ribs. Moving a baby in utero was top on my list of things I never wanted to try, but my husband was a physician. He was the only person, aside from my O.B., who I trusted to do it.

"Better?" he asked.

Joey darted toward the kitchen, probably to get an ice pack for me. Tierney's aerobics were that regular an occurrence.

"Yes," I breathed. Deep down, I felt a popping sensation, then a rush of moist heat. My eyes widened. "Oh, shit."

"What?" he asked, hands already on my stomach. "She already wormed her way back?"

"No." I sighed. "My water broke."

The color drained from Levi's face. "Are you sure?" he gasped.

"I'm pretty freakin' sure," I said through my teeth as a contraction gripped me.

He jumped up. A twinge of jealousy rippled through me, that he could move that way. "How did you miss the contractions?"

I scowled. "I had human *feet* kicking at my ribs, Levi!"

"Touché." He glanced around the room. "Where are my keys?"

"We are *not* taking the Tesla." I heaved myself up from the couch. "Joey!" I called. "Grab your baby bag. We're dropping you off at Auntie Pamela's. It's go time!"

"But where are my keys?" Levi asked again.

Joey bounded into the living room, the keys to my car in his hand. "It's go time, Daddy!"

Breathing through the contractions, I directed my husband to where I'd stashed what I'd taken to calling our baby bags, then shepherded him and our son out to the car.

"You're not driving!"

"Of course I'm not." I tossed him the keys. "I'm *never* doing this again."

"Until Pamela gets knocked up again and you start craving another baby."

Another contraction ripped through me. I shot him a glare. "Shut up and drive."

He helped me into the car, pressing his lips together to contain a laugh. "You're a terrible parental figure right now."

"I'll show you terrible," I said through clenched teeth.

"Daddy, really." Joey buckled himself in. "Don't test her. According to one of Nan's books, childbirth is blackout-level painful."

"Childbirth," I muttered. "I'm about to push out a bowling ball through a balloon hole."

We pulled into Pamela's and Theo's driveway. Grabbing his bag, Joey climbed out of the car. I pushed my door open, and he came to my side for a hug and kiss.

"Give your cousin kisses for me," I said, "and be good." Pamela and Theo's three-month-old daughter was the cutest thing, with light brown skin and curly red hair. I couldn't believe that, in just a few hours, I'd be welcoming my own daughter into the world.

"I will!" Joey kissed my cheek, then darted to the front door.

"Um," Levi said.

"What?"

"Did we let them know we were on our way?"

"No," I howled through yet another contraction. Tenacious Tierney was coming at me, fast and furious.

The door swung open. A confused Pamela glanced down at Joey, then out at us in the car. "Go time?" she called.

"Go time!" I gasped in response.

"Enjoy the drugs!"

Levi floored it to the hospital. As we sped down the highway, I texted my parents. More than likely, my mom was working on the surgical floor, but she could come to the maternity wing after her shift. Nothing made me happier than our newfound, close relationship.

The next few hours sped by in a blur of contractions, dilation announcements, and Levi pacing, then it really was go time. A year earlier, if someone had told me that I'd be back in the delivery room, giving birth to our second child and re-married, I would've laughed at them. Ever since Levi proposed again, though, everything had fallen into place—even with Tierney's ninja-like arrival into our lives.

I'd self-published my novel and, even though I was nowhere near quit-my-job status, I'd taken the first step. Levi was thriving at the clinic and, with it, Joey gained an entire library of reading material. Our son was going to cure Lupus or something, and our daughter, well . . . maybe it was the childbirth, but she was going to kill me.

Both the painkillers and the high that came only with labor kicked in, though, and the rest of Tierney's delivery was easy. At least, that's how I remembered it. Someone once said to me that women forget birth pains after the baby comes, and it's true.

I stared into her sweet face, wrinkled and pink, my head resting against Levi's shoulder. After a little while, Pamela and Theo arrived with their daughter and Joey. Laying there with my family surrounding me, I couldn't think of a time when I'd ever been more content. And it was only the beginning.

With our family between us and the ground firmly beneath us, Levi and I had a lifetime of adventures and happiness ahead of us.

Levi leaned over our daughter, his eyes reflecting my thoughts as he rested his forehead against mine. "No more stairs," he said.

"No more stairs," I agreed.

I sought his lips with mine, pouring every ounce of peace and contentment from my heart into Levi as we kissed. For the rest of my life, I'd wake up in our bed with him beside me.

The life I'd wished for all those years was finally mine. All we needed was a dog.

The End

ACKNOWLEDGMENTS

They say it takes a village to raise a child. It also takes a village to birth a book.

Well, we did it—my thirteenth novel is out in the wild. I've dubbed it #LuckyNumber13 because I finished editing it during tornadoes and thunderstorms. We so rarely get twisters here in Connecticut; it figures one would touch down practically in my backyard.

It seems like it gets harder every time even without tornadoes, but I'm fortunate to have many people who helped me along the way.

My biggest thanks to you, dear reader, for taking a chance on me and spending your time in my little book baby's world. I appreciate every moment you give me. *You* are why I do this.

In no particular order, I also have to thank the following people.

My reader group, Barone's Belles, for being my safe haven and hot doctor GIF central.

Blaine McCrea, for giving me "Bapa."

Robin Masiewicz-Morehouse, for naming Stems & Ivy Classical Learning Academy.

Shoutout to my sister-in-law, Britt Campbell, who is the other half of our niece's auntourage—two aunts who follow her around and fuss over her.

Brea Cameron, Samantha Ardito, Kelly Pestritto, Crystal StClair Angus, and Angela Rose Hebert for settling the bath vs shower debate. You have no idea how much I agonized over that before you all shared your thoughts with me.

My critique partner Molli Moran and beta readers J.C. Hannigan and Robin Leaf, for making me better with your notes and reaction comments. Now we just need to be able to embed GIFs in comments . . .

Elizabeth Ann West and the What Authors Need to Know group, for your support and encouragement.

Natasha Snow, for the cover of my heart.

Last but not least, Mike, for giving me every morning for the rest of forever.

STAY IN TOUCH

Sign up for Elizabeth Barone's newsletter to get book updates and exclusive bonus content.

Visit *elizabethbarone.net/newsletter*

WHAT TO READ NEXT

JUST ONE MORE MINUTE

Rowan peered into the oven, her hand guarded by a thick oven mitt. The scent of chocolate wafted toward her. Though the brownies *smelled* done, the slightly chocolate-coated toothpick in her free hand told her otherwise. "Just one more minute," she decided. Pushing the pan back inside, she closed the door.

Brownies were hardly a healthy dinner, but she'd had a long night at work. Usually she didn't mind her job waitressing tables at the diner. Sean's regular crowd gently teased her but left generous tips. But Sean's was also right off the highway, and every once in a while they got drunk strangers. Her soiled clothing was currently cycling through its second run in her old washing machine. After being vomited on, anyone would need a good dose of chocolate.

And wine.

Maybe it was a sign that she needed to get out of waitressing. The problem was, she had no idea what she should do instead. She'd finished her A.S. in May. Given her experience, she could apply for a management position at a restaurant. The pay would be decent, but she just wasn't sure that she wanted to work holidays and weekends for the rest of her life.

Sighing, she turned away from the oven and grabbed her

notepad. With a swipe of her pen, she adjusted the time on the recipe that she was working on. In the three years since she'd started her blog, she had yet to post a recipe for brownies. She was about to remedy that.

Her blog was also an option. Because of it, she earned a pretty decent side income. Between affiliate sales and paid product reviews, she was able to pay her rent, and her waitressing income took care of her bills and other expenses. Now that she was out of school, if she quit her job and focused on her blog full-time, she could easily turn that income into a living. The idea of sitting in her kitchen all day didn't really appeal to her, though. She liked bantering with her customers at Sean's. Though her readers left great comments and busted her balls just fine, it wasn't the same as face to face interaction.

She had no idea what she wanted.

The timer on her oven went off. Her minute was up. She pulled the pan of brownies out of the oven and set it on top of the burners of the stove. Immediately she turned the oven off. Despite the sun having set hours ago, the temperature outside hovered in the upper eighties. It was going to be a brutal summer.

The brownies had to cool before she could cut them, so she left the oven and ambled into her living room area. As she crossed the small studio, she glanced at a photo on the wall of her aunt Katherine. Her heart twisted. She hadn't seen her aunt in two years. They talked on the phone occasionally, but things weren't the same. Too much was unspoken between them.

Closer to the air conditioner, she felt the sweat on her face drying. She sat down on her futon, tucking her legs underneath her. She drummed her fingers on her thigh. She didn't have cable, and opening up her laptop and surfing YouTube would only make her feel guilty that she wasn't working on her blog post instead. She bit her lip. Maybe it was time to get cable.

Her phone vibrated against the worn coffee table. Frowning, Rowan leaned forward for it. It was almost midnight. She didn't recognize the number. Silencing the phone, she figured someone had probably dialed wrong—it happened.

Almost a minute later, a notification flashed across the screen. One new voicemail. Her frown deepened.

Rowan's bad luck streak gets worse when she inherits a bakery with the guy who stole her dream job and broke her heart.

Purchase via elizabethbarone.net or your favorite retailer.

ABOUT THE AUTHOR

Elizabeth Barone is an American novelist who writes contemporary romance and suspense starring sassy belles who chose a different path in life. Her debut novel *Sade on the Wall* was a quarterfinalist in the 2012 Amazon Breakthrough Novel Award contest. She is the author of the **South of Forever** series and several other books.

When not writing, Elizabeth is very busy getting her latest fix of Yankee Candle, spicy Doritos chips, or whatever TV show she's currently binging.

Elizabeth lives in northwestern Connecticut with her husband, a feisty little cat, and too many books.